Praise for *In His Place*

"Through masterful character development, tight writing, and a fast-paced narrative, Harry Griffith packs the pages of *In His Place* with complexity, poignancy, and truth. The reader weeps to consider the failure of the Church to incarnate Jesus for a lonely old man and then watches as the Body of Christ finds it faith, its feet, and its courage. That Christlike courage is contagious and transformative, but it doesn't happen in the 15 days recorded in the novel. It happened over 15 years of invested ministry by a pastor who came to understand the truth that to live is Christ and to die is gain."

—Carmen Fowler LaBerge, President, Presbyterian Lay Committee Chairman, Common Ground Christian Network

"I highly recommend *In His Place*, first as a novel with vivid human interactions by (mostly) likable characters who are thrown into situations that test their Christian commitment. Aside from enjoying the novel, however, I have been unable to shake the question raised by an atheist friend of the pastor. When a lonely member of the parish takes his own life, the atheist wants to know how anyone who belongs to a church can be so alone. *In His Place* poses a challenge for all church-going Christians. Are we really acting in His place?"

—Charlotte Hays, coauthor of *Being Dead Is No Excuse*, frequent contributor to the *National Catholic Register*

"On one occasion, while driving through my hometown in the Atlanta suburbs, I felt a strong inner urge—no, a push—to stop and offer a ride to man with a briefcase. He got in and told me where he was heading. I noted it was a long way to walk. He said it was, but he had Parkinson's and could not drive. On arrival, he got out and said, 'You just did for me what Jesus would have done.' An unforgettable moment! This book's premise is just that—If we live 'in Him' life will be remarkable and so fulfilling. I encourage you to read it."

—Victor Oliver

"Along with justification by grace through faith, the indwelling Christ was Paul's core understanding of the Christian faith and way. Living a life IN CHRIST is the nature of Christian discipleship. That means we are primarily responsible not TO Christ, but FOR Christ. We are to live as Christ in the world. In this attention gripping novel, *In His Place*, Harry Griffith provides an exciting picture of one man seeking to live "in His place." If you will read the first few pages, you will not want to put it down; but more important, reading on, the core meaning of Christian discipleship will become crystal clear."

—Maxie Dunnam, Former President, Asbury Theological Seminary and former World Editor of *The Upper Room*

"There are a number of surprises in this first novel by Harry Griffith. First the positive and honest portrait of a sincere, but very human, pastor. One sees that so seldom in the media and modern literature. Next crisis after crisis suddenly appear and take both the pastor and the reader by surprise and move the plot along with increasing tempo. Lastly, mixed in throughout the book, we find theology and practical challenge for both the individual Christian reader and for any Christian congregation. By all means give this book a read and take the challenge."

—Rt. Rev. John H. Rodgers Jr. (Retired), Dean/ President Emeritus Trinity School for Ministry

In His Place

A Modern-Day Challenge
for Readers of *In His Steps*

Harry C. Griffith

SHILOH RUN PRESS
An Imprint of Barbour Publishing, Inc.

Print ISBN 978-1-63409-766-6

eBook Editions:
Adobe Digital Edition (.epub) 978-1-63409-848-9
Kindle and MobiPocket Edition (.prc) 978-1-63409-849-6

This book is a work of fiction. Names, characters, places, and incidents are either products of the author's imagination or used fictitiously. Any similarity to actual people, organizations, and/or events is purely coincidental.

Published by Shiloh Run Press, an imprint of Barbour Publishing, Inc., P.O. Box 719, Uhrichsville, Ohio 44683, www.shilohrunpress.com

Our mission is to publish and distribute inspirational products offering exceptional value and biblical encouragement to the masses.

ecpa Member of the
Evangelical Christian
Publishers Association

Printed in Canada.

Acknowledgments

This book would not have been possible without the help of Jim Pence, Julie Cosgrove, Victor Oliver, Bruce Barbour, Greg Johnson, Ronald Rolheiser, Barry Grecu, John Rivenbark, and my ever-supportive and encouraging wife, Emily.

Additional support came from Maxie Dunnam, Fitz Allison, Keith Miller, George Gallup, Robert Whitlow, Cecil Murphey, Peter Lundell, Ron Hooks, Charlotte Hays, Kacky and Joyce Avant, and Bob Snyder.

Prologue

Otis Huntington sat at a rickety wooden table and picked up a small brown bottle of sleeping pills. His hands trembled as he fumbled with the childproof cap, working it back and forth. Finally, the cap popped off and fell to the floor.

Instantly, the *click, click, click* of tiny paws sounded on the grimy tile floor. Otis's little Yorkie-mix mutt came over and sniffed the cap.

"You leave that alone, Skeeter. Y'hear?"

The scraggly wire-haired dog let out a quiet whine.

Otis poured the bottle's contents into his palm.

About twenty-five pills. More than enough.

He held the pills in the palm of his hand as if weighing them and then dumped them back into the bottle. He couldn't take them yet. He didn't know how quickly they would take effect, and there were still two things to do.

Otis jotted down a quick note on a piece of paper torn from a yellow legal pad then sealed it in an envelope.

He took the envelope, along with a roll of duct tape, and walked across to Mrs. Sherwood's apartment. He pulled his knobby sweater closer to his chest as the rush of autumn air whistled through the breezeway.

He tore off two short lengths of tape and secured the envelope to her front door, just below the metal numerals 212. Otis wasn't worried about waking her up. Mrs. Sherwood slept like the dead. She'd find the envelope when she came out to get her newspaper tomorrow.

Otis ran his fingers along the door frame's peeling paint. He absentmindedly pulled a few large chips loose and let them flutter to the floor, where they joined the others. The whole building needed repainting. Not his problem now.

When Otis returned to his apartment, Skeeter jumped and danced as if he hadn't seen him in months. It never ceased to amaze Otis how much this little dog seemed to love him. He picked him up and cradled him in his arms.

"You'll be all right now. She'll take good care of you."

One final task remained. Otis sat back down at the table and pulled the legal pad to him. He took his pen and began to write.

Dear Pastor Steve. . .

Chapter 1

I sat on the bed and rested my head in my hands.

Jayne laid her hand on my shoulder. "I'm so sorry," she said softly. She bent down and kissed my cheek and then left me to my thoughts.

As I pulled on my sneakers, my mind replayed the phone call I had just received.

"Is this Pastor Steve Long?"

"Yes."

"This is Officer Robb with the Belvedere Police Department. Is Otis Huntington a member of your church?"

A wave of anxiety shot through me. "Yes, he is."

"We need to contact his family. Do you know any of his relatives?"

"Otis has no family." I cleared my throat, changed the phone to my other ear. "Is something wrong?"

There was a slight pause.

"Mr. Huntington was found dead in his apartment this morning."

For a few seconds, I couldn't reply. Then I choked out the words. "What happened?"

"That's still under investigation. Would you be able to come down to the hospital and identify his body?"

I swallowed hard, fighting back the emotion that flooded to the surface.

"Sure. I'll be there in about twenty minutes."

As a pastor, I had made many trips to the hospital to be with people when they were dying. And I had gotten my share of late-night phone calls telling me that a member of my congregation had died. This was the first time I had been asked to identify a body. But that's not what bothered me.

Jayne came back in, carrying coffee in a stainless steel travel mug.

"Thought you might need this," she said, handing me the mug.

"Thanks." God had chosen a great wife for me. She always anticipated my needs.

"Did they say what happened?"

I shook my head. "Only that it's under investigation."

Jayne's eyebrows furrowed. "Who would've hurt that sweet man?"

"I don't think anyone did. I'd better get over there."

I grabbed my keys and started for the door, but Jayne caught me by the arm. "Are you okay?"

I shook my head. "Not really."

It doesn't take long to get anywhere in Belvedere, Georgia. From the city center, where Jayne and I lived, Belvedere's limits were about five miles in any direction, give or take a mile. So it only took me about ten minutes to get to the hospital.

I wheeled my pickup truck around the back of the hospital, toward the ER, and into one of the parking spots marked CLERGY. A Belvedere police cruiser was parked nearby.

Like the city where it is situated, the Belvedere Hospital is small. Only four stories. And no big morgue like you see on TV. As a matter of fact, bodies are usually sent to Atlanta for autopsies. So I didn't have to trek down to a basement and wait for a medical examiner to dramatically open a stainless-steel door and roll the deceased out of a drawer.

A uniformed police officer met me in the emergency room. His name tag—Robb—identified him as the one who had phoned me.

"Officer Robb," I said, "I'm Stephen Long."

We shook hands.

"Thanks for coming, Reverend. He's down here."

We walked down a short hallway and entered Treatment Room D.

Otis lay on the table, partially covered by a sheet. He looked peaceful.

Officer Robb looked at me, arching an eyebrow and shifting from one foot to another.

I nodded. "That's Otis," I said. "Can you tell me what happened?"

"Well, as I told you on the phone, it's still under investigation, but right now it looks like a suicide. There was an empty bottle of sleeping pills on the kitchen table."

"Did he leave a note?"

Officer Robb shook his head. "Only instructions about caring for his dog. He taped those to a neighbor's door, along with a key to his apartment. She's the one who found him. She came out to get her morning paper and saw the envelope. The note didn't say anything about suicide, though. Just asked her to take care of the dog. She got worried and decided to check on him. When he didn't answer the door, she went in and found him."

Officer Robb switched directions. "You sure he doesn't have any family we can contact?"

"I'm sure. He's been coming to our church for about a year now, and he told me early on that he was alone in the world. He asked me to handle the arrangements if something ever happened to him. Told me there wasn't anybody other than Skeeter."

"Skeeter?"

"His dog."

Officer Robb nodded. "Funny thing about that dog," he said. "He was curled up with him in his recliner when his neighbor found him. He wouldn't even leave his side when she knocked at the door." He nodded toward Otis's body. "Looks like the dog was his best friend in the world."

Those words stung. They were more accurate than the officer knew.

I sat down on the grass, on a hill just outside the hospital, watching traffic on the four-lane road that bisected Belvedere. Most of the town's new growth spread toward the west, near the interstate. The east part of town was older, although most North Georgia towns preferred the term *historic*. I had to admit, it sounded better than the more accurate descriptions: *run-down, abandoned, deteriorating, low-income*.

But one thing that the east and west parts of town had in common was Loop 121. It was the main east-west artery through town, and there was hardly a time of day when it wasn't busy. Almost constantly, cars, pickups, and eighteen-wheelers rushed back and forth on this road, speeding toward their various destinations.

This spot had always been special to me. I could look to the north and see the mountains in the distance, peaceful and beautiful. I could look below me and see the hectic pace of everyday life. Somehow the balance between the two—calm in one direction and frenetic in the other—represented for me what life is all about and helped me cope with it.

As I sat there, watching the traffic, thoughts and "what-ifs" raced back and forth through my head like cars and trucks on Loop 121.

Why'd you do it, Otis?

If there was one person in the world I would have thought incapable of suicide, it was Otis Huntington. Although a quiet man who kept to himself, Otis never appeared to be unhappy. I saw him from time to time during the week while he did his maintenance work at the church and then virtually every Sunday, but I never picked up a hint that he might be suicidal.

In fact, Otis seemed to be one of the happiest people I knew. He didn't have much in the way of material things, especially compared to the congregation of Incarnation Church, but that didn't seem to bother him. Our church was upscale for a small-town congregation. In that sense,

Otis didn't fit in very well. He didn't dress as nicely. Most of the time he came to church wearing clothes he'd gotten from Goodwill.

But the people were always kind to him. Nobody treated him badly because he didn't fit into the proper income bracket. The church used some of its benevolence fund to help him with his bills from time to time, and I had hired him as church groundskeeper and maintenance man when he'd lost his other job.

Otis never complained. He always seemed to be in good spirits, and his positive attitude encouraged others. He never failed to talk about the Lord in his life, both in the church and outside. It was a natural thing with him. I have no idea how many people he personally led to the Lord. He certainly moved me closer to Christ.

So what went wrong? What could have pushed Otis over the edge so radically that he saw suicide as his only option?

Otis lived in the Southern Plantation apartment complex, an elegant, but absurdly inaccurate, name. The place looked nothing like that, unless perhaps Tara after the Union troops burned it.

It was one of the three oldest complexes in Belvedere,

and its age showed everywhere you looked. Potholes dotted the deteriorating pavement. All the buildings were in need of new roofs, and the amber paint peeled so badly that a sprinkling of chips littered the ground around most of them.

But the age of the complex was the least of its problems. Southern Plantation was a center of the illegal drug trade in Belvedere. The police were regular visitors to the complex, and the calls were not social.

That was quite a contrast with most of the people from Incarnation Church. Those who did go on visitation were reluctant to go to the Plantation, as they called it. Maybe they were afraid they wouldn't come out in one piece. I had made many visits there, and the thought had crossed my mind more than once.

But today as I pulled into a parking spot in front of Otis's building, fear for my personal safety was the furthest thing from my mind. I wanted—needed—answers, and I hoped that somewhere in Otis's little apartment I might find them.

The police had completed their investigation by early afternoon and released the scene. I had a key because Otis had asked me to be the executor of his estate several months earlier. Why hadn't that given me a clue to what was going on in Otis's mind?

"Shouldn't be too hard," he'd told me. "I don't have much of anything."

He wasn't kidding about that.

I stood in the front room, looking for something but not knowing exactly what.

The tiny one-bedroom apartment was neat but sparsely furnished. An old brown sofa, leaking stuffing from the armrests, sat up against one wall of the living room. A recliner covered in a sickly shade of green vinyl occupied the opposite corner. That was where Mrs. Sherwood found Otis, according to the police.

On the kitchen table lay an assortment of bills and envelopes, carefully organized. Beside them a yellow legal pad provided a checklist of paid bills and disconnected services. Another list gave bank account details and access information. A third page contained funeral arrangements.

It was as if Otis had carefully considered each issue that someone would have to consider in dealing with his death. Otis had taken care of every detail—except one. He hadn't left an explanation.

I spent several hours going through the apartment, looking for some hint that would help me understand what happened. I found nothing. I was about to go home when

I heard a knock at the front door. I opened it and found a thin African American woman standing there holding Skeeter in her arms. As soon as Skeeter saw me, he started wiggling and whining. The woman put the little dog down, and it ran into the living room and hopped into Otis's green recliner.

"Look at that," she said. "Poor thing misses him so."

I held out my hand. "I'm Steve Long. Otis's pastor."

She nodded and shook my hand. "I'm Lonetta Sherwood. Otis told me a lot about you."

"Mrs. Sherwood, I'm struggling to understand this. Did you notice anything unusual about Otis the last few days? Anything at all?"

She shook her head and dabbed at her eyes with a lace handkerchief.

"I saw him yesterday afternoon, and he seemed fine. He told me he was going on a trip."

"Trip?"

She nodded. "And when I found the envelope on my door this morning, asking me to take care of his dog, I thought he'd just forgotten to mention it. Well, he didn't say how much to feed Skeeter, and so that's why I knocked on his door. He didn't answer, so I tried the doorknob." Her eyes filled with tears. "That's when. . ." She brought the handkerchief to her mouth and choked back a sob.

I shook my head. "I'm baffled and desperately want to understand exactly what happened. Did he really use the word *trip*?"

"Not exactly," she said. "He told me he was going to see his best friend."

As I left the apartment complex that day and headed back to the church, her words resonated through my mind.

He told me he was going to see his best friend.

Otis had revealed his planned death to her as casually as if he were announcing his vacation travel plans. An eerie feeling crawled down my spine that told me I would soon learn why Otis took his own life, and I wouldn't like the answer. How could I prepare the congregation for the news?

Chapter 2

The letter arrived in the church mail, one day after Otis's death. It swept over me with the force of a tsunami.

Betty Ferguson, our church secretary, brought it to me with several other pieces of mail. The envelope was hand addressed in Otis's unruly scrawl. I tore it open and pulled out a sheet of yellow legal paper, obviously taken from the same pad he'd used to make out his final to-do lists. On the paper, Otis wrote:

> Dear Pastor Steve,
>
> I want to thank you for all you've done for me.
>
> I'm sorry for doing this. I know I'm letting you down. I've tried to hold on, but I just can't stand the loneliness anymore.
>
> I know Jesus will forgive me.
>
> I'm tired, and I want to go be with Him.
>
> Love,
> Otis

Loneliness? The word jolted me. Otis was an active member of our church. He was there every time the doors were open. How could a dear guy like Otis have been lonely?

A flood of guilt washed over me, followed by a host of what-ifs. What if I had spent more time with Otis? What if I had probed a little deeper the last time I saw him looking sad? What if I had visited with him the day he called me. . .the day before he killed himself? I ran a mental check of my last few interactions with him, but I couldn't think of a single thing that might have tipped me off to his intentions.

Nevertheless, the guilt remained. Why didn't I make Otis a priority? Why wasn't I more proactive with him? And how was it possible for someone to be a member of Incarnation Church and yet feel lonely and isolated? Most of all, where could I find answers to all of these questions?

Every pastor needs a confidant, someone outside his church with whom he can share his deepest frustrations, hurts, and questions. Someone he can go to when the wheels are coming off and everything around him is falling apart. Someone he can trust not to give him the easy answer but to show tough love.

There is a problem with confiding in other pastors. As strange and ungodly as it may seem, there is often competition between the clergy in any town. Any problem we have can seem like a weakness when we consider sharing it with another pastor. You would think that other pastors would be the logical ones with whom to share your concerns because they can be expected to understand your trials and tribulations, but I was reluctant to do it. Pride.

Philip Treadway wasn't a pastor. In fact, he wasn't even a practicing Christian. He was a guy who had faced disappointment with God and wanted nothing to do with the church. Yet, strange as it may seem, I felt more comfortable talking to him than just about anyone other than my wife.

When Jayne and I first came to Belvedere, Incarnation Church was not in good shape financially, and for a time I had to be a bivocational pastor. Philip Treadway was good friends with Incarnation's board chairman, Clifton Stoner. Clifton knew that Philip needed someone to help at his lumberyard and set up a meeting between us.

"Who knows? Maybe you'll be able to get him to come to church," Clifton said, winking. "He hasn't been inside one for twenty years. Not since his boy was killed by a drunk driver."

I don't know exactly what it was, but Philip and I hit it off from the moment we met. Maybe it was his sardonic, humorous outlook on the world. Or perhaps it was because he sharpened me by challenging my assumptions and beliefs. For whatever reason, it wasn't long before Philip was more than my part-time boss; he was my best friend.

Several years ago, the church raised my salary to the point where I didn't need a second job. But even though I no longer worked at Philip's place, that was where I went when I needed to process things.

I knew two things about Philip. One, he would tell me the truth. And two, I could trust him.

Philip Treadway smiled at me from behind the counter as I walked through his little store. I was constantly amazed at his ability to stay in business in this day of places like the mega home improvement chains that take up a city block. Yet despite these gargantuan competitors, his lumberyard plugged along and continued to turn a profit. The building was long and narrow, had no air-conditioning, and showed its age everywhere. There wasn't much flash, and Philip catered primarily to contractors rather than do-it-yourselfers.

Of course there was something else that Philip's business offered that the big boys couldn't quite match. There was a friendly, you might say homey, atmosphere at

Treadway Building Supplies. When you went into Philip's store, it was more like going to the local café. There were three stools in front of the counter at the back of the store, and usually one was occupied by a contractor, a salesman, or just somebody who stopped in to visit. And there was always coffee.

Philip Treadway was a large man. I am fairly tall, but standing next to him, I looked short. With his muscular build, shaved head, and goatee, he also looked like he could be a bouncer. In spite of this, I had never met a gentler giant.

Philip stood, and his massive hand swallowed mine when we shook hands.

"Haven't seen you in a while," he said. "I thought maybe you'd forgotten about me. What brings you here today?"

"First things first," I said as I sat down on a stool. "Coffee."

"It's been busy. You get the dregs today." He poured a cup of coal-black liquid from a nearly empty carafe and handed it to me.

I took a sip and shuddered.

"Powerful stuff, huh?" he said with a grin.

"Much more of that and I won't sleep for a week."

"So what's up?"

I looked down into my Styrofoam coffee cup and back

at Philip. "One of our members committed suicide."

Philip winced and shook his head. "Who?"

"Otis Huntington."

Philip knew many of the people at Incarnation Church. He knew Otis particularly well. Otis had worked for him for several years.

"I'm sorry. Did he leave a note?"

I handed Philip the letter. "This came in today's mail."

Philip's brow furrowed as he read the note. "Does the rest of the church know?"

I nodded. I had called Clifton Stoner, the board chairman, the night before and asked him to pass on the news.

"How are you handling it?" he asked.

"Not very well."

Philip shook his head. "That's not what I mean. How are you going to handle it with the congregation? How are you going to explain it to the church at the service tomorrow?"

"Explain it?"

"Look, I'm not trying to be sarcastic, but isn't suicide a major no-no for you guys? Do you really think that people aren't going to put a negative spin on this? Look at it as a failure on Otis's part?"

"Why would they blame Otis?"

"So they don't have to blame themselves."

Philip was my friend, but he had touched a raw nerve. I

raised my hands. "Look, man, I didn't come in here to start an argument. I'm still processing this myself."

"I know that," he said, not letting my response ruffle him. "But this is something you need to think about. You're the pastor. The buck stops with you. When you stand behind your pulpit tomorrow, your congregation is going to want answers. They're going to want you to tell them that Otis's suicide is not their fault."

I raised my voice. "It isn't their fault." *Why do I feel so defensive?*

"Are you sure of that?" Philip shot back. "Are you certain that the church did everything it could to prevent this?"

I felt my face flush. "How could we prevent something we didn't even know about? Otis never told me or anybody else that he planned to kill himself."

Philip paused and pierced me with his gaze. "Didn't tell you? Or couldn't?"

"What do you mean?"

He leaned across the counter. "All I'm asking is this: How can a man like Otis be a part of your church yet die of loneliness?"

Chapter 3

I didn't want to admit it, but Philip was right.

I drove back to downtown Belvedere and pulled into Incarnation Church's parking lot. I sat in my truck for a few minutes, mulling over what Philip had said. How was it possible for someone to be an active member of our church yet die of loneliness?

Incarnation Church, with its tall spire and stained glass windows, overlooked downtown like a silent sentinel. The church had a rich history. Our building was a registered historic landmark and had stood in downtown Belvedere for over one hundred years.

But had it become nothing more than a shell? Had it ceased to be a place of healing? A place where people could come to connect with God? A place where they could worship and find community? More importantly, a place of changed lives, of people radically committed to Jesus Christ as Lord and Savior? A body of disciples?

I walked into the sanctuary and sat down on the

burgundy-colored, carpeted steps that led up to the platform. I deliberately left the house lights off, allowing only light from the stained glass windows to illuminate the room. A colorful mosaic of red, yellow, green, blue, and violet sunbeams splashed along the pews and the carpeting.

I've always been a bit of a traditionalist, so I loved Incarnation's handcrafted windows. They were not original to the building. The church imported them from England in the 1940s. Beginning with the annunciation to the shepherds and concluding with the ascension of Christ, they told the Savior's story through stunningly beautiful artwork.

Over the years I had served as pastor of Incarnation, this is where I came when I needed to talk things over with God. The mute splendor of the stained glass quieted my spirit so I could listen to His Spirit.

I got up and walked down the left side of the sanctuary, pausing at each window, contemplating the story each told. One of my favorites was Jesus healing the leper. The man knelt before the Savior, a pleading expression on his face. His words echoed in my mind.

"If You are willing, You can make me clean."

Jesus' arm was outstretched, His hand touching the man's head.

"I am willing; be cleansed."

To reach out and touch an untouchable was unthinkable. But Jesus did it.

I moved on to the feeding of the five thousand. The window depicted Jesus standing, surrounded by a multitude. He held a piece of bread in one hand, a fish in the other.

"I have compassion on the multitude."

In the next window, a woman washed Jesus' feet with her tears and dried them with her hair. How scandalous that would have been.

I went from window to window, walking through the life of Christ and thinking about each incident depicted, until I came to the final—and most majestic—window. This window, which loomed behind the platform twice the size of any others, was the only one that held a caption.

As Jesus ascended into heaven, the disciples stood on the Mount of Olives, gazing up at Him. The expressions on their faces were a mixture of wonder and fear. The caption read: As THE FATHER HAS SENT ME, I ALSO SEND YOU.

I read the caption several times, tossing it around in my mind.

"I also send you."

Those words attached themselves to my mind and wouldn't let go. Why did they have such a hold on me? What did it mean?

Chapter 4

*A*s the Father has sent Me, I also send you."

Even though it was a Saturday and I had already prepared a sermon, I knew I had to throw it out and start from scratch. That meant I wouldn't be home on Saturday afternoon as usual. I pulled out my cell phone and called Jayne.

"Hello?"

"Hi, sweetheart. Just wanted to check in and let you know I'm at the church."

"Aren't you coming home for lunch?" she asked.

"I'll grab something down here. I've got to work on my message for tomorrow."

Silence filled the other end of the line. This was out of character for me, and she knew it. More silence on her end. After an uncomfortable pause, I heard her take a deep breath. "What's up? You okay? You always complete your sermon on Friday so you can take Saturday off." I could sense concern in her voice.

"I need to rework it. Otis's death has changed things."

A hint of concern colored her reply. "Are you sure you're all right?"

"I'm fine." I hoped my tone shielded the doubts in my mind.

Tomorrow's sermon would be very different from the norm. I decided that Incarnation Church's Sunday morning service would double as Otis Huntington's memorial service. He had no family other than the church, and he'd left all the details for the service in my hands.

I hoped and prayed this service would be a life changer for me and for my congregation. In any case, I knew I owed it to Otis—and God—to get it right. I had to say what needed to be said without playing on people's emotions. The congregation's grief was genuine, and a reflection of my own. But I wanted my message to be uplifting rather than depressing. Striking the right balance remained the challenge.

I had no idea what the results would be. Even though Incarnation had endured some financial struggles over the years, it nonetheless continued to be an affluent church. Our members were the doctors, lawyers, and business executives of the area. Would they receive what I had to say? I knew I was about to have a test case when Clifton Stoner, our board chair, dropped in.

Stoner was not a big man. He stood about five foot

four and probably weighed 130 pounds. But his thick mane of white hair and piercing blue eyes gave him a stern, austere appearance. Even though he was a banker, he reminded me of a judge.

I learned early on in my tenure that Clifton was Incarnation's "church boss." If he didn't sign off on something, it didn't happen. The rest of the board, as well as the congregation, would go whichever way the wind blew. And Clifton Stoner was the wind.

Stoner opened the door—he never knocked—entered my office, and sat down in one of the two plush leather chairs that sat in front of my desk.

I leaned over the desk and shook his hand.

"Terrible thing about Otis." He shook his head.

I nodded.

"When's his memorial service going to be?"

"Tomorrow morning." I tented my fingers.

Clifton's brow furrowed, and he sat up straight. "During church?"

I nodded again.

Stoner looked down at the floor and shook his head. "I don't think that's a good idea."

"Why not?"

"People come to church on Sunday to worship and be encouraged. It's not the time for a funeral."

"On the contrary." I opened my hands. "I can't think of a better time. This church was the only family that Otis had. And I think we let him down."

Clifton gave me a sharp look. "What are you talking about?"

Otis's note lay on my desk. I pushed it over toward him. "Read this and see what you think."

The yellow legal paper shook in Stoner's hand as he read it. He folded his arms across his chest after he put the paper back on my desk.

"And this means what?"

"Our mutual friend Philip Treadway put it to me this way." I cleared my throat. "How could Otis be an active member of your church and yet die of loneliness?"

Leaning across the desk, he glared at me a moment and wrinkled his forehead. "Look, we're all concerned about Otis's death and the way it happened, but you can't be suggesting that we could have done anything to prevent it. Are you saying we were too high and mighty for Otis? That we made him feel inferior to the rest of us?"

"I'm saying that maybe we all could have done a better job of ministering to him."

"That's ridiculous!" Stoner clamped his jaw and gave me that piercing look that commanded the attention of so many.

"Calm down." I raised my hands in a defensive posture. "I'm not pointing fingers. I'm guiltier for what happened than all the church put together." My words caught in my throat. I paused for a moment, trying to collect myself.

"Otis called me the day before he killed himself, wondering if we could get together for a few minutes. I told him I was in the middle of my sermon preparation and asked if we could postpone it for a day or two. I could hear something in his voice. Something that should have tipped me off that he needed help. But I ignored it.

"I keep thinking that if I'd just taken the time to meet with him, he might still be here. Do you have any idea how that makes me feel? I'm supposed to be a spiritual leader, but I didn't have the sensitivity to hear the desperation in Otis's voice.

"Or maybe I did hear it but just didn't want to inconvenience myself, or—"

Clifton interrupted, his voice softened. "Otis's suicide wasn't your fault either, Pastor."

"Maybe not directly," I said. "But I still feel that I should have done more to help him, to at least listen to him."

Clifton didn't respond. Finally, I broke the uncomfortable silence.

"Look, I'm not planning to use the memorial service to beat up on anybody. But I think that it's the least we can do for Otis. We're the only family he had."

Clifton looked unconvinced. "What if we have visitors?"

"Then I hope they'll be impressed that we cared enough for one of our own to take the time to show him our love and respect."

Clifton cleared his throat loudly but said nothing, spun out of his chair, and left in a cloud of anger.

Chapter 5

Am I just rationalizing? Am I planning to force my thoughts on the congregation and don't want to admit it?

Late afternoon eased into evening, and once more I stood alone in the front room of Otis's little apartment. I'm not sure what drew me back there. After standing up to Clifton Stoner and telling him that I planned to use the Sunday morning service as a memorial for Otis, I got this sinking feeling that I had just grabbed a tiger by the tail.

Clifton Stoner could be a powerful ally, but he was an even more menacing adversary. Over my fifteen years at Incarnation, we had been at odds more than once. And during that time, I had learned to choose my battles carefully. Maybe that was why I found myself back at Otis's place. I wanted to make sure this was one of those battles in which I needed to engage. I also wanted to reassure myself that I wasn't using Otis's death as an excuse for pushing my own agenda.

One thing was certain. If I followed through with my plans for tomorrow, there would be no turning back.

As I began to thumb through Otis's books and papers one more time, the doorbell rang. I opened it and found Otis's neighbor, Lonetta Sherwood, standing there holding Skeeter.

"I hope I'm not bothering you." She looked out toward the street. "I saw your truck out front."

"Not at all." I opened the door. "Come in."

Mrs. Sherwood entered the apartment and set the little dog down. The same as last time, Skeeter immediately hopped up into Otis's recliner. Mrs. Sherwood shook her head and smiled sadly. "He's still so lonely."

"So you've adopted him?"

"That's what I wanted to talk to you about. I'm touched that Otis would trust me to take care of Skeeter after he— well, you know. But I work full-time, and there's no one here during the day. I wondered if someone in your church might be a better companion for him."

"Well, I, uh." My mind searched for a polite way to decline.

"I'd hate to take him to the pound, but I'm afraid that's

what I'll have to do if I can't find a home for him soon."

I knew resisting was no use. "I, uh, guess we can take him until we can find a home for him."

A look of relief came over her face. "Thank you, Reverend. Looking after his little dog isn't much, but it's the least we can do for Otis, isn't it?"

"You're right, Mrs. Sherwood. It's the least we can do."

She shook my hand once more and then left me alone with Skeeter. I picked up the scruffy little dog and sat down in Otis's recliner. He curled up in my lap and breathed a contented sigh.

"So, what am I going to do with you?"

Maybe I should do what Mrs. Sherwood didn't want to do. I would pass Animal Control on my way home. It would be easy enough to leave Skeeter there and be done with it. It wasn't that I didn't like dogs. I just didn't need something else on my plate right now.

I glanced over at the small table beside the recliner. On it were Otis's Bible and a worn copy of Charles Sheldon's book *In His Steps*. It had been many years since I had read the book, but there was no way to forget the classic question it posed: "What would Jesus do?" Frankly, I had a problem with the WWJD thing. Granted, it wasn't wrong to use Jesus as a model for our actions, but surely there was more to the Christian life than just asking ourselves that question every time we faced a decision.

"As the Father has sent Me, I also send you."

Those words rang in my head all day, but now others joined them.

"As long as I am in the world, I am the light of the world."

Jesus spoke those words to His disciples, but He also told them, *"You* are the light of the world." Great words, but how are they supposed to play out in real life? I hated to admit it, but at the moment I had no idea.

I glanced down at the little dog sleeping in my lap then up at Otis's wall clock. It was late, but Animal Control would still be open. A wave of guilt washed over me, but I tried to push it out of the way.

"Come on, Skeeter. Let's go."

Chapter 6

How could one little dog be the source of such emotional distress? I must have circled the block around Animal Control at least five times before I finally admitted I couldn't leave Skeeter there. Whether it was God or an overactive conscience that stopped me, I couldn't tell.

"This is stupid," I told myself. "It's just a dog. It shouldn't be this difficult."

All reason and logic were on my side. The parsonage was owned by the church, and there was a no-animals policy we had to abide by. Besides, adding an animal to the household would create a whole new set of dynamics we didn't need right now. Furthermore, we could also do without the extra expense of caring for a dog, as fetching a little guy as he seemed to be. Wouldn't Skeeter have a decent chance at being adopted by a loving family?

Yet every time I looked at the little dog on the seat beside me, I saw Otis's face. I saw a man I had let down, a man who had died of loneliness. A man who might possibly still be alive if I had been more in touch. One of his last wishes was that his dog might be properly cared for. How could I ignore that?

Nevertheless, that's exactly what I tried to do. On my last lap around Animal Control, I even pulled into the parking lot and sat there for a good ten minutes.

It was no use. At least for now, Otis's little dog would become a member of the Long family. Unfortunately, he would have to be a stealth member because of the church's no-pets policy.

It used to be a common practice, but nowadays it's quite rare for a church to provide a parsonage for its pastor. But Incarnation is an old church. And their parsonage is an old house. Nestled in one of the older neighborhoods of Belvedere, our two-thousand-square-foot bungalow did not reflect the wealth of the church that owned it. Not that it was run-down, but neither was it in perfect condition. In fact, parsonage repair frequently made it onto the agenda of church board meetings. Over the past five years, I had painted it, replaced the roof and the carpeting, and made major repairs to the plumbing and wiring. Sometimes I amused myself by speculating on whether the church had hired me because I am a handyman rather than for my preaching and pastoral gifts. Still, it was a decent place to live and a good neighborhood for our children to grow up in.

I kept reminding myself that I wasn't in pastoral ministry for the money or the perks. I tucked Skeeter under my arm as I climbed our front porch steps and entered the house. It didn't take long for my children to notice our new arrival.

"A dog!" screamed Hannah, our eleven-year-old, as she bounded across the living room. Hannah is a little sprite and a chatterbox, with dark hair like mine—though hers is usually in a ponytail—and a face that likes to smile. "Is he ours? Can we keep him?" She turned and yelled down the hall toward the bedrooms. "Brandon, Dad got us a dog!"

Brandon, our fourteen-year-old, called out from his bedroom. "No he didn't." Brandon is blond like his mother and, though quiet by nature, was always a typical first child and older brother—steady, responsible, and dependable—that is, until he became a teenager. Then it was as though some wires snapped and he became self-absorbed, insolent, and unreliable. At least that's how it seemed when he was around me.

"Yes, he did," she shouted back. And before I could say a word, she scooped up Skeeter and ran down the hallway to prove her point.

About that time, I looked up and saw Jayne standing in the doorway to our small dining room. She didn't say a word. She just looked at me with raised eyebrows.

Jayne was the glue that held our little family together. She was a strong-willed decision maker, especially regarding family issues. She whispered so only I could hear her, "I hope you know what you're doing."

With my legs apart as though standing on solid ground and my hands making the motion of being on the level, I said, "It's temporary, just till we can find him a home."

Jayne nodded toward the kids' bedrooms. "Try telling them it's just temporary."

"Yeah, well, there wasn't much I could do. Otis's neighbor foisted him off on me before I had a chance to explain all the reasons it wouldn't work."

As if on cue, Brandon and Hannah came into the living room. Brandon carried Skeeter now. "I thought we weren't allowed to have a dog."

"Skeeter belonged to Mr. Otis." I gave them a "Dad means it" look. "He'll only be staying with us until we can find him a home."

Brandon handed the dog back to his sister. "Told ya," he added over his shoulder as he left the room.

Hannah shot him a withering glance and held the wriggling dog tightly. "Why can't we keep him?"

"Honey, you know the church doesn't allow pets in their house."

"But it's our house, too." Her bottom lip trembled as tears welled up in her eyes. "It's not fair."

"Maybe not, but you can at least enjoy him for a little while."

"I don't want him for a little while," she sobbed. "I want him to be mine forever."

"Listen, Hannah—" I began, my voice rising, but Jayne interrupted.

"Hannah, I think Skeeter probably would like to have something to eat. Why don't you see if he likes some of the leftover rice from last night's supper?"

Hannah nodded and brushed away the tears as she led the little dog into the kitchen.

Jayne called after her, "Not too much now. And give him some water, too." Then she came over, put her arms around my waist, and kissed me. She took me by the hand and led me toward the front door. "Let's go out on the porch."

I can't say enough good things about this wife of mine. I could pull a lot of lines from Proverbs to describe her wisdom, kindness, and strength of mind, emotion, and spirit. She's the rock of stability in our little family. She's also a beautiful blond, tall and stately.

When I think of how fortunate I am to have Jayne as my wife, I'm reminded of something that happened years ago. I ran into a friend who had known Jayne and me in college. I told him I had just met his wife, Cindy, and that we had something in common. He replied with a laugh that we had both out-married ourselves. My sentiment exactly!

It was particularly at times when I was perplexed that I valued this wonderful woman the Lord had let me have as a partner in life. And now was one of those times.

The sun began to set and a cool breeze washed over us as we sat down on the porch swing.

"I'm sorry." I looked to the horizon and sighed. "I didn't mean to start World War Three."

"She'll be fine." She took my hand. "How are you doing?"

I shook my head. "Not so good. I can't shake the feeling that Otis's death is my fault, at least in part. I guess that's why I brought the little guy home. Maybe I'm doing penance."

"You can't think that way. Otis made his own choice. That wasn't anyone's fault. Certainly not yours."

I shrugged. "It's not just Otis. I just can't get past what Philip said. How can someone be a member of our church— an active member—yet die of loneliness? What are we doing here if we're not reaching out to people like Otis?"

Jayne leaned up against me and rested her head on my shoulder.

I kissed the top of her head.

She didn't say a word.

Didn't need to.

Chapter 7

Daddy, why did Mr. Otis die?"

Hannah's question took me by surprise. For most of the evening, her only topic of conversation had been Skeeter. She'd proposed every conceivable scenario by which we could keep him and by which she would be able to have her very own dog. I could, of course, have called Clifton Stoner and asked for at least a short reprieve from the no-pets policy, but there were too many crosscurrents of dispute going on right now. I didn't want to add to them. So, one by one, I'd had to shoot down her ideas.

No, we couldn't convince the people in the church to change their minds.

No, we couldn't hide Skeeter and pretend we didn't have a dog.

No, we couldn't make him an outside dog.

When she ran out of arguments, she melted down and went back to her bedroom crying.

Skeeter accompanied her.

The battle had gone on all evening, so when I went to say good night, I expected another onslaught. Instead, she asked the one question I wasn't prepared to answer. How do you explain suicide to an eleven-year-old?

She lay on her bed, covered by a pink, quilted comforter, her dark hair splayed across the pillow. Skeeter, obviously sensing his primary advocate in the house, had curled up on the bed, tight up against her.

"Well, sometimes people get very, very sad, and they decide they don't want to live anymore."

"Did he shoot himself?"

"No, what gave you that idea?"

"That's what Brandon said."

I made a mental note to have a talk with Brandon as soon as I left Hannah.

I brushed my fingers through her hair. "No, sweetie. He took some pills that made him go to sleep."

Her brow furrowed. "But why would he leave Skeeter?"

"He didn't. Not really. He asked his neighbor to take care of Skeeter, but she wasn't able to. That's why I brought him here, so we could do what Mr. Otis wanted and find a home for him."

Hannah was quiet for a long moment. "Did Mr. Otis go to hell?"

Her words shot through me like a lance. "Did Brandon tell you that, too?"

She nodded.

"No," I said. "Mr. Otis loved Jesus. I imagine he and Jesus are sitting together right now, having a long talk."

She looked at me with blue eyes, big enough to melt the hardest of hearts. "Are you sure we can't keep Skeeter?"

"No, sweetie, we can't. But I'll tell you what we can do. We'll take our time finding a home for him. You'll get to enjoy him for a good long while. Now, go to sleep. We have a big day tomorrow."

Hannah smiled and closed her eyes.

The handmade sign on Brandon's bedroom door read: "Knock, please. If u don't, I bust ur face."

Not that I was worried, but I knocked anyway.

"What?" His somewhat surly voice called through the wooden barrier of his self-made sanctuary.

"It's Dad."

A few seconds later, the door opened partway. Brandon stood there in a T-shirt and pajama pants, blocking the entrance. At fourteen, he was nearly as tall as my almost six feet, but his straight blond hair and fair complexion favored his mother.

"May I come in?"

Brandon stepped away from the door and walked back to his desk. He put a headset on and focused his attention on a flat-screen monitor. I had evidently interrupted a game of Halo 3.

"Could we talk?"

Brandon nodded.

"Without that?" I pointed to the monitor, where someone had just blown up.

Brandon sighed and paused the game. He turned and looked at me as though I weren't there.

"Hannah seems to have gotten the idea that Otis shot himself. Do you know anything about that?"

A look of surprise flashed across Brandon's face. "Didn't he?"

"Why would you think that?"

"He killed himself. I just thought—I mean, isn't that how most people do it?"

I shook my head. "Otis took an overdose of sleeping pills."

"Oh."

"Did you also tell her Otis went to hell?"

Brandon nodded and looked down into his lap.

"Why would you say that?"

He shrugged.

"Look at me."

Brandon looked up, his expression a mixture of sorrow and defiance.

I repeated my question, a bit more firmly. "Why would you say that?"

His jaw muscles worked, as if he were biting back his reply.

I reached down and pulled the Xbox power cord from the wall.

"Hey!"

"You got your sister pretty worked up tonight. You need to learn to think before you talk, son. You're grounded from video games for a week. What is happening to Otis right now is up to God, not you or me. Maybe you need some time to think about what you said to Hannah."

Brandon stood up, his hands balled into fists. "That's not fair!"

I wrapped the cords around the Xbox and tucked it under my arm. "Neither is life."

I set the Xbox down on the dining room table.

Jayne pointed to the video game. "What's that all about?"

"Do you know what he told Hannah?" My anger still quaked in my voice. "He told her Otis shot himself. And then he told her Otis went to hell. He's lucky all I did was take away his Xbox."

"Did you talk to him about Otis? About what he's feeling?"

That stopped me in my tracks. Why had I not been willing to talk through Otis's death with my son? Why had that thought never even occurred to me?

Jayne poured two cups of coffee and handed me one.

"He's been quiet all day," she said. "I think he's taking Otis's death pretty hard."

Her words hit me like a two-ton weight. Ever since I had received word about Otis, I had been running around, tending to arrangements, talking to everybody but my own kids. And in the process I had managed to forget that Brandon probably had been closer to Otis than anyone in our family, including me.

Otis worked as the church groundskeeper, and as soon as Brandon was old enough, Otis asked if he could hire him as a part-time assistant. The powers that be on the church board nixed the idea, so I worked out a compromise. Brandon worked with Otis on Saturdays, and I paid him myself. My son had been working as Otis's helper every week for the better part of a year, but I hadn't taken the time to reach out to him, to see how he felt about Otis's death.

I tucked the Xbox back under my arm and headed back toward Brandon's room.

No light shone under the door.

Surely he didn't go to bed this early.

I knocked softly.

"Brandon? Are you awake?"

No answer.

Was he asleep or did he just not want to talk? I waited a little while, trying to decide what to do. *Maybe sleep is the best thing for him right now.* I leaned the Xbox up against the door.

I'll talk to him tomorrow.

Chapter 8

S unday morning didn't begin well.

Sometime during the night, Brandon retrieved his Xbox from outside his bedroom. I knew I had to talk to him—apologize for last night—but with my mind so fixed on the memorial service, I couldn't concentrate on anything else.

I left for the church long before he got up.

I began that Sunday morning, hoping to use Otis's death to awaken the congregation to who they were and who God wanted them to be in Christ. Maybe not the best plan I could have come up with. All I knew was that I wanted to challenge them to incarnate Christ to the world around them and to explain to them what I meant by that.

I was realistic about how much support to expect. I had no grand vision that the entire congregation would rush forward and commit themselves to a radical expression of

Christianity. At a guess, a 10 percent response would be a success.

If I could just persuade a solid nucleus of folks, I would be happy.

Instead, I alienated almost everyone.

The memorial service was low key. There was no casket because Otis had donated his body to science. Instead, Jayne placed an eight-by-ten framed portrait of Otis on the communion table. He'd also requested no flowers, asking that any money be given to Incarnation's missions fund. Even so, there were a few wreaths at the front of the sanctuary. My friend and Otis's former employer, Philip Treadway, had sent a particularly large spray.

When I looked out over the pews, I was pleased to see Philip seated in the back row. It was probably the first time he had stepped inside the door of a church in more than a decade.

As for the congregation, I couldn't take their temperature, and that made me nervous. Usually I can gauge how people respond by reading their expressions. But for the most part, the people looked stone-faced.

I hadn't picked up any gossip about the "real" reason Otis killed himself. Nor had I heard any talk about how scandalous it was to have a church member commit suicide.

And some of the people seemed genuinely sad.

Halfway through the service, we had an "open microphone" time for people to come up and share stories about how Otis touched their lives. The silence that followed quickly morphed from uncomfortable to awkward to embarrassing. That's not unusual. People find it difficult to stand before a large group and talk about personal feelings. But eventually a few came up and said some nice things about Otis.

As I got up to speak, my hands were clammy and my mouth was dry. I felt like a seminary student giving his first sermon in homiletics class. I had lost count of the number of funerals I had presided over in fifteen years as pastor here, but I had never felt like this.

Was I worried about what I was going to say?

Or about how they were going to respond?

Too late to be concerned about either. I had something to say, and I was going to say it, regardless of the consequences. I gripped the pulpit and looked out over a church full of people.

"Otis left detailed instructions for his memorial service," I began. "And he specifically requested there be no eulogy. Nevertheless, it's customary at a memorial service for the pastor to offer some words of comfort to the family.

"But Otis had no family, aside from us.

"And I'm not sure how much comfort I can or even should offer. Rather than this being a time for that, I think it needs to be a time for soul searching. Indeed, the best way to bring meaning from Otis's suicide is by learning something from this tragedy."

I unfolded the letter that Otis sent me.

"I want to read something to you. This letter is from Otis. It arrived a day after he died."

Dear Pastor Steve,

I want to thank you for all you've done for me.

I'm sorry for doing this. I know I'm letting you down. I've tried to hold on, but I just can't stand the loneliness anymore.

I know Jesus will forgive me.

I'm tired, and I want to go be with Him.

Love,

Otis

As I read the letter, I glanced briefly at the congregation. I could tell by the expressions on their faces that Otis's words were making an impact. What kind, I wasn't sure.

"This letter broke my heart." I squelched my emotions. "Otis called me the day before he died, wanting to talk. I was busy that day, and I put him off. Maybe I didn't pick up on the desperation in his voice. Or maybe I didn't want to inconvenience myself.

"Whatever the reason, I failed Otis.

"Shortly after Otis's death, someone asked me a question I couldn't answer. And that question's been haunting me ever since."

I gripped the pulpit as if it were about to fly away from me and then spoke softly but clearly.

"How is it possible for someone to be a member of Incarnation Church and die of loneliness?

"I can't wrap my mind around that. Were none of us close enough to Otis to help him when he needed it most? Was there nobody in this church he could talk to or confide in? As church groundskeeper and custodian, Otis ministered to us in many ways.

"Why didn't we minister to him?

"We're an affluent church, yet Otis lived in a rent-assisted apartment. We go out to fine restaurants, but Otis got by on food stamps. We have our social circles. However, Otis's best friend was his little dog, Skeeter.

"Is it possible that we, in our comfort and prestige, never let Otis join the club? Is it possible that we worshiped with Otis every week but never invited him into our lives? Is it possible that he embarrassed us?"

I shook my head and looked down at the pulpit.

"I don't have an answer for that."

My next words caught in my throat, and I had to pause before I could get them out. "Why do we gather here each week if not to be the expression of the body of Christ? And if we are the body of Christ, how did we let someone like Otis slip through the cracks?

"There is a famous quote by Teresa of Avila, a Christian of centuries ago. She said, 'Christ has no body now on earth but ours. Ours are the only hands with which He can do His work. Ours are the only feet with which He can go about the world. Ours are the only eyes through which His compassion can shine forth upon a troubled world.'

"Our name is Incarnation Church. We are the body of Christ collectively. And I've come to believe that as individual Christians, we are called to incarnate Jesus Christ to the world personally.

"The incarnation of Christ—Christ among us here on earth—did not end when Jesus ascended into heaven. Jesus said, in the Gospel of John 20:21, 'As the Father has sent Me, I also send you.'

"Jesus is living in our day and is doing the things He did when He walked this earth. He is doing them through those Christians who are willing to accept the responsibility to be who they are called to be as followers of Christ.

"We're not just to respect Christ. Anyone can do that. We're not just to imitate Christ in the sense of asking ourselves, when faced with a choice, 'What would Jesus do?' We're here to incarnate Christ, to let Him live within us by His Holy Spirit to affect everything we do.

"That's the kind of Christians I want us to be."

As I surveyed the congregation, my heart sank. I saw only two people who were clearly connecting with my message—my wife, Jayne, and Clifton Stoner's wife, Flora.

I held up my hands, as if apologizing. "Look, I'm not here to cast blame for Otis's death, and I mean that. I am challenging all of us, the people of Incarnation Church, to learn to live with and in the presence and power of God.

"I want us to be Jesus to the world around us.

"Now, you might be sitting there thinking that your pastor's crazy, that I've gone off the deep end and become some kind of nut. That's okay.

"But for those of you who are willing to begin to live as Jesus lived, we will meet in the fellowship hall at eleven forty-five."

Then I made the mistake of quoting Matthew 11:15, "He who has ears to hear, let him hear!" In retrospect, it must have sounded self-righteous to some and insulting to others.

I closed in prayer and stood at the back to greet the

people. I received the usual "Great sermon" and "I enjoyed that" comments. But quite a few people didn't say a word as they left.

Their eyes, however, spoke volumes.

It was eleven thirty by the time everyone had left the sanctuary.

Jayne took Brandon and Hannah home, and I hurried over to the fellowship hall to see how many had accepted my challenge.

I sat at a table in the empty fellowship hall.

The wall clock read eleven forty-five.

A couple of hundred people had attended the memorial service and heard my "incarnation challenge."

Not a single person had responded.

I decided I would give it a few more minutes when I heard a voice behind me.

"No one's coming. You know that, don't you?"

I didn't need to turn around. I knew Clifton Stoner's voice all too well.

Clifton walked across the large room and stood beside my table.

"You really hurt yourself today, Pastor. I told you not

to get on a soapbox, but you couldn't resist. If you want people to follow your leadership, you can't throw mud at them. I had no idea what was going on with Otis. Neither did they.

"We each carry our own burdens and can't be nurse-maids to every down-and-out person who has a problem."

I was about to respond when another familiar voice chimed in.

"You're wrong."

This time, I did look around.

Clifton Stoner's wife, Flora, stood in the doorway.

A tall, imposing woman with silver hair and a regal appearance, Flora Stoner was one of the kindest, most gracious women I have ever known. Although she and Clifton were easily the wealthiest couple in the church, she remained unaffected by her social status. In fact, if anyone in the church already lived out the life of Christ day by day, it was Flora. Flora Stoner was one of a handful of people in the church I could always count on for help, even if the job was tedious and unglamorous. She wasn't afraid to get her hands dirty and serve others.

Flora came over and rested her hand on my shoulder.

"Don't let the blame fall at your feet alone, Stephen. Many of us knew"—she shot a glance at her husband—"or should have known, what was going on with Otis. And you're right. We did nothing."

Stoner shook his head and flipped his right hand, dismissive of his wife's remarks. "The fact remains, nobody's taking you up on your challenge. What do you plan to do now?"

I shook my head.

"I don't know."

Chapter 9

In years gone by, when people in a church were displeased with their pastor, they would gossip about him behind his back. Occasionally you'd hear rumors, most often coming from a "friendly" parishioner who said something like, "I thought you ought to know what so-and-so is saying about you."

Those were the good old days. In the era of modern technology, the preferred method of delivering pastoral criticism is via e-mail. It is a much more efficient means of letting an errant minister know he has crossed a line. No need for a potentially uncomfortable face-to-face. A quick e-mail or text message, with a cc addressed to key elders or deacons, of course, would do the trick.

Now a pastor can be roasted at the speed of light. I had barely walked in the parsonage door when my phone buzzed. The text was short and to the point.

IT WAS UNFAIR OF YOU TO BLAME US FOR OTIS'S DEATH.

I didn't think I had quite blamed anybody for Otis's

death, but evidently some took it that way. I know I used Otis's death as a way to challenge them to go deeper spiritually, and I wasn't being Christ to them by closing with that "ears to hear" remark, but I wasn't willing to admit I totally messed up.

More e-mails and texts flooded my phone, most all of them variations on the same theme. By the time I had walked from the front door to my home office, the general opinion of my incarnation challenge was fairly clear, and it wasn't good.

As the day went on, messages continued to trickle in like hand-counted election results. In all fairness, the response wasn't entirely negative. But even those who "supported" the idea did so from the safe position that this would be a great thing for someone else to do. The senior citizens felt I had given a great challenge to the young people. The younger crowd thought my ideas could best be implemented by the older folks. The parents with young children said it would be a great thing to do—someday.

With each e-mail, each text, each social media message, my mood darkened a little bit more. I felt like Elijah must have after Jezebel threatened his life. Elijah ran and hid, but then he asked God to let him die. He was convinced that he was the only one of God's prophets left.

I didn't have the luxury of running away and hiding. And although I was depressed, a death wish was over the top.

But I honestly thought about resigning.

I was in my twenty-fourth game of computer solitaire by the time Jayne brought me a grilled cheese sandwich and diet cola. The sky outside my office window had changed from rich blue to a splash of gold and red.

"I thought you might be getting hungry." She handed me a tray. "You've been in here all afternoon."

"Thanks." I took the food and set it on my desk.

"You coming out anytime soon? The kids would like to see their dad for a few minutes today."

I kept staring at the card game on my monitor. "A little later, maybe."

"Hanna's taught Skeeter some tricks. She'd like to show you before she goes to bed."

I nodded as I dragged the ace of hearts to the upper left of the screen.

Jayne came up behind my chair and massaged my shoulders. One of the things I loved about her was that she knew when her touch would be more powerful and comforting than her words.

"I've been here fifteen years. You'd think that by this time I'd at least have a few people who would follow my leadership." I dragged a four of clubs onto one of the columns of cards on my screen.

"You do."

I looked up at her. "Name one."

She hesitated.

"I thought so."

"How about me?"

"You're the pastor's wife. You don't count."

"Flora Stoner, then."

Jayne was right. Flora Stoner was as strong a supporter as I had ever had in the church, not to mention that she was Jayne's dearest friend. Unfortunately, her husband, Clifton, was the biggest thorn in my side.

"She and Clifton cancel each other out."

"Don't be so sure about that. Flora can have a pretty strong influence on Clifton when she wants to."

I nodded. "Okay, I'll give you that. But she's still just one person."

"There are others. They might not be vocal, but they're there."

I shook my head. "I don't know if I can do this anymore."

Jayne didn't say anything. She just leaned down and kissed me on the cheek. She knew me better than anyone else. And she'd heard me say those words before. Jayne knew arguing was pointless. For one thing, I rarely meant it when I talked about resigning. It was my way of wallowing in self-pity. Usually, after a day or so, the sun would come out and the clouds of depression would evaporate. All would seem right with the world, and I would be eagerly planning some other way to reach the world.

"Would you like some coffee?"

I squeezed her hand and gave my head a slight nod.

After she left, I turned my attention back to my game of solitaire. Not that I cared that much about the game. It was a mindless diversion. Something I didn't have to think about, but that would—or so I thought—keep my mind off my troubles.

Truth is, it wasn't helping much. If anything it allowed me to wallow in my self-pity all the more. About five minutes had passed when Hannah came in, carrying my stainless steel travel mug, full of steaming coffee. She was dressed in pink pajamas, and her hair was still damp from her bath.

Skeeter trailed after her.

"Here, Daddy." She held the mug out to me.

I wheeled my desk chair around to face her. "Thanks, sweetie."

I was about to turn back to my computer when I noticed that she and Skeeter still stood there.

"Was there something else?"

Her voice was quiet, almost shy. "Can I show you the trick I taught Skeeter?"

I smiled. Jayne had set me up. "Sure. Let's see it."

Hannah had a cube of Colby cheese in her other hand. She turned and faced Skeeter, holding the cheese in front of the little dog. She instantly had the dog's full attention. Her face grew serious as she held up one finger. "Skeeter, sit."

Over the next few minutes, the little dog jumped, bounced, rolled, barked, and did everything imaginable except sit. Hannah finally gave up in frustration and handed Skeeter the cheese.

Deflated, Hannah looked at me and said, "He did it before. He really did."

"I believe you. Come here." I held out my arms. Hannah sat on my lap and put her head on my shoulder. She smelled of perfumed soap and shampoo.

I could have sat there all night.

For those brief moments, all troubles were forgotten as I reveled in the presence of my little girl.

Out of the blue, she posed a question to me. "Does Skeeter miss Mr. Otis?"

"I'm sure he does, sweetie. When I was over at Mr. Otis's apartment, Skeeter kept jumping into Mr. Otis's recliner and hunkering down. I think he wonders where his friend went."

"Can we keep him?"

I kissed the top of her head. "No. The church doesn't allow animals in their house."

"It's not fair. Can't you make them change their mind?"

No, I thought. *Seems like I can't influence them about anything anymore.*

"I wish I could, honey."

"Can't we move somewhere else?"

"And where would we move?"

"Somewhere that would let us keep Skeeter."

"I'd have to change jobs for that."

She gave me a look that said, "Well, could that happen?"

Little did she know how close she was to getting her wish—about my changing jobs, that is.

I kissed her once more. "You'd better start getting ready for bed. School tomorrow."

"Yuck." She frowned and stood up. "Come on, Skeeter," she said in a huffy voice. Both girl and dog went from my office with, psychologically speaking, their tails between their legs.

A few seconds later, Jayne reappeared at my door. A conspiratorial grin spread across her face.

I waggled a finger at her and tried to hide my smile. "You set me up."

"I thought you needed a Hannah fix. Now, why don't you go talk to Brandon?"

"How's he been doing today?"

Jayne shook her head. "Quieter than usual. He's hurting, but he's keeping it bottled up." She came over and kissed me. "Like someone else I know."

"And what makes you think he's going to open up to

me? Particularly after last night."

"You won't know till you try." She kissed my forehead. "Go talk to him."

I sighed, dragged myself out of the office chair, and went up the stairs one slow step at a time, as though I were climbing a mountain. *Why do I find it so difficult to talk to my son?*

I stood in the hallway outside Brandon's room. I knew Jayne was right. I needed to talk to him, to try to draw him out and help him deal with his grief. But I had been such a jerk the night before, now I didn't have a clue how or where to begin.

Give me a hundred angry deacons and I'm fine. But when it comes to one sullen teenage boy, I'm tongue-tied.

I knocked on his door.

No answer.

I knew he was in there. I could hear the explosions coming from his video game.

I knocked again—a little harder.

"Brandon?"

"Yeah?"

My mouth went dry.

"Just wanted to tell you good night."

"Okay."

I walked down the hallway toward my bedroom.

I'll talk to him tomorrow.

Chapter 10

Dawn broke cold, rainy, and drizzly. I sat on the front porch drinking a cup of coffee, listening to the rain, and trying to read my Bible. At least my eyes were moving over the page. But my Monday morning mood did not allow for focus on spiritual things.

Sometimes pastors call them blue Mondays. This one felt like a black one. I kept going over the Sunday service in my head, trying to figure out how my sermon could have offended so many people. Maybe I transferred to the congregation my own guilt about not being more attentive to Otis. Maybe I expected too much of them. How could they really know how Otis felt? It's just that we were not a very diverse group at Incarnation, and I wondered if lower-income people felt unwelcome. In the midst of us, Otis died of loneliness. But I had spoken from my heart and been as honest as I could. I had never been a particularly confrontational person, and maybe that's what shook up so many people.

As I sat on the porch swing, the drizzle increased to a steady rainfall.

There haven't been many times when I had no idea what to do or where to go next, but today was one of those times. I went for broke yesterday, challenged people to a different view of the Christian life, but it seemed to have fallen on deaf ears.

My *"He who has ears to hear, let him hear!"* words came—unwelcome—back into my mind.

What does a shepherd do when the sheep won't follow him anymore?

Maybe it's time to hand them over to a different shepherd.

I would have sat there on the porch and brooded all day if Jayne hadn't come out to sit with me. She brought my travel mug filled with steaming coffee. Jayne was keenly aware of my moods and always knew when I needed a kick in the pants to get moving.

"So are you going to sit here all day?" she asked. "I think that's what you did yesterday," she added.

I sipped the hot coffee, surveyed the rain as it dripped off the roof, and glanced at her before answering, "Looks like it."

She shook her head. "Nope."

I raised an eyebrow at her.

"You're going to drive the kids to school today."

I took a deep breath and let it out, as if she had just asked me to perform a gargantuan task. "Can't you do it?"

Jayne nodded. "Of course I can. But you are doing it today."

"Why?"

"Because you still need to talk to Brandon. You can't keep putting it off."

"It takes all of fifteen minutes to drive both of the kids to school, and Hannah is with us for half that time. You expect me to get Brandon to open up about Otis's death in seven minutes? I'm not that good a counselor."

"You don't need to get him to open up in seven minutes." She tilted her chin in a way she knows makes my knees buckle. "All you need to do is show him that you care, that you understand that he's hurting, too."

I shook my head. "Seems like every week he gets harder to talk to. It's like I don't even know what to say to him anymore."

"All the more reason to try." Jayne dropped the car keys into my lap. "Talk to your son." She turned and went back into the house.

I sighed, took the keys, and called through our screen door. "Come on, kids, time to go to school."

Hannah bolted out the door before I finished my sentence. She wore a Red Riding Hood raincoat and practically bounced her way out to the minivan.

Brandon was another matter. I waited before calling again. No need to get the morning started off on even worse footing. But after a couple of minutes passed, I called again. "Brandon, we're going to be late."

Brandon strolled down the hall, as if he were trying to go as slowly as possible. He wore holey jeans and a ratty T-shirt. His hair was a mess, and he had earbuds in his ears with a cord leading down to an iPhone.

Based on his expression, his mood appeared worse than my own.

He walked past me and out the front door.

"Brandon," I called. "Aren't you forgetting something?"

He turned around and looked at me. "What?"

I gestured toward the rain, which had now become heavier.

He looked at me as if to say, "Yeah? So, what?"

"You're going to get soaked."

He rolled his eyes and shook his head dismissively then walked through the rain to the van.

This is going to be a fun fifteen minutes. I took another sip of coffee and followed him.

The first half of the drive actually was fun. Hannah's school was closer, so we dropped her off first. She sat up in the front with me while Brandon sat as far back in the van as he could. Hannah talked the whole time, mostly about Skeeter and the different tricks she planned to teach him when she got home from school.

After I watched Hannah run up the sidewalk to Dean Rusk Middle School, I adjusted my rearview mirror so that I could see Brandon. His head rested against the window, and his eyes were closed. Though not asleep, he was certainly absorbed by whatever blasted from his iPhone. How could I possibly engage in a conversation with him when I felt more like a chauffeur than a dad?

I called over my shoulder, "Brandon."

No response.

I yelled a little louder. "Brandon!"

Then I noticed his noise-canceling earbuds still jammed in his ears. If his music was cranked up as loud as he usually had it, I could yell all day and he'd never hear me.

I was about to put the van into PARK, lean back, and try to get his attention when a horn sounded. Behind me, a line of cars with frustrated parents and bouncing kids stretched half a block.

Wouldn't have been able to talk about much in five minutes anyway. I sighed and pulled back out into traffic.

When we were stopped at a red light a block away from the high school, Brandon miraculously regained consciousness.

"I'll get out here," he said as he lurched for the door handle.

I looked into the rearview mirror. "What?"

Brandon's hand was already on the side-door handle. "I'll walk the rest of the way."

"It's pouring. You'll get soaked."

He shrugged and stepped out into the downpour. "I'll be okay."

"Brandon," I called after him, but he slid the door shut before I could say another word. As I watched him turn and walk down the block toward the school, I called out above the rush of raindrops, "I love you, son."

From dropping Brandon off at the high school, I drove on to the church. Like many pastors, I normally take Mondays off. Sundays can be so physically and emotionally draining I'm not of much use to anybody the next day. On those occasions when I've tried to work, I've been like an author in the grips of terminal writer's block. I stare at a blank computer screen for several hours, allegedly working on next week's sermon. But by noon, I've rarely even been able to decide on a topic or text. So I've usually decided that I might as well stay home and vegetate on Mondays.

Today was different. I still felt like vegging, but I needed to process what had happened yesterday, to try to figure out what I had done wrong. I needed to come up with a plan B, since plan A didn't motivate anyone.

And the church was the best place to do that. It was the one place I could be sure I wouldn't be disturbed. Everyone knew I didn't keep office hours on Mondays, so if people needed me, they called the parsonage land line or my cell phone. But they never dropped by the church.

I could ignore the phones and leave the building locked and dark. It would be my private retreat today. At least, that's what I thought.

But the whole complexion of the day changed when I pulled into the parking lot and saw Clifton Stoner's black Cadillac Escalade sitting there.

I groaned and almost decided to drive back home. But I realized that Clifton wouldn't be at the church unless he'd already learned from Jayne that I wasn't at home. If I went home, he'd just follow me there sooner or later.

I pulled into my parking place, said a quick prayer, and entered the church.

Chapter 11

Down the hallway, I could see light coming from my office.

The lion waited to pounce.

I wasn't up to a confrontation this morning, particularly with Clifton Stoner. But since Clifton had not left me the option of avoiding him, I headed for my office, steeling myself for the onslaught I knew was coming.

One final quick prayer and I opened the door.

My day brightened instantly.

Flora Stoner—not Clifton—waited for me. A wave of relief swept over me, kind of like when a police officer pulls you over and you're afraid you've been caught speeding, only to learn that a brake light isn't working. Flora didn't remind me of a police officer, but she did bring back wonderful memories of my first-grade teacher who seemed to care about me despite my rebellious attitude about attending school.

I guess that was appropriate, as she'd spent more than thirty years as an elementary school teacher. And even now she volunteered at the high school. Kind and gracious, with just a hint of command in her, Flora Stoner earned respect, even from the toughest teenagers.

She sat at my desk writing a note on a legal pad as I entered the office.

"Flora, aren't you supposed to be at the high school?"

She looked up from her note. "Oh good, I can tell you in person."

"Tell me what?"

"Sit down, Stephen." I knew this was serious. Her formality with my name got my attention.

In what felt like a strange reversal of roles, I sat down in one of the brown leather armchairs that faced my desk. Now I really did feel like I was sitting in front of my first-grade teacher. Thankfully, she got up and moved to the other armchair, across from me.

Flora leaned forward in the chair, gave me a stern look. "You stand firm!"

When she saw my puzzled expression, she continued.

"What you said yesterday. Your challenge that we need to be Jesus to the world around us. Don't let anybody pressure you into backing away from that. No matter what they do, you stick to your guns."

I gave her a weak smile. "Do you know something I don't?"

She started to wave the question off but then answered,

"Clifton and some other board members have been talking. They're planning some sort of response to your challenge yesterday, and it's not a positive one. I'm not sure what they're going to do, but don't you let them intimidate you.

"You have the right idea, and you need to keep pressing forward. If we all had the courage to incarnate Jesus to the world around us, there's no telling what we could do."

I smiled. "Thanks for the vote of confidence, but other than Jayne, you're the only one I seem to have persuaded."

Flora shook her head. "Not so. There are others. You'll see. They just need time to process it. And they need an example." She pointed at me. "That's you. But if you give up, we'll all just go back to being Sunday Christians and coasting through this life."

I nodded. Flora Stoner was a difficult person to argue with. "I'll do my best."

"That's all anybody can ask." She stood up. "Now, I'd better get over to the high school. I don't want to get in trouble for being late," she ended with a wink.

"You're a volunteer." I grinned. "What are they going to do? Dock your pay?"

She held up a finger. "Still, we must set a good example."

I took her hand. "Thank you."

She put on her stern teacher look again. "Just hang in there, young man."

"You make me feel better already." I cocked my head. "It's been a long time since anyone has called me 'young man.'"

Flora laughed. "Compared to Clifton and me, you and Jayne are practically children."

We walked down the dark hallway toward the exit. "Well, this child has two of his own to care for, and one of them is a full-blown teenager." My voice revealed my frustration.

As we went outside, the rain had stopped, so I continued with Flora over to her car. "Do you get to see Brandon much? Is he doing okay?" I scuffed the pavement with my shoe, hands deep in my pockets. "I mean, is he getting along? Does he have friends? Switching from homeschooling to public high school has been a big change for all of us."

Flora nodded and patted my hand. "He's doing just fine. Relax." Her keyless entry beeped.

I chuckled as I held the door open for her. "Easy for you to say. Your kids are all grown."

From the driver's seat of her Escalade, she gave me her most confidence-inspiring look. "And as you can see, we survived the teenage years. You will, too."

I closed her door and waved as she drove off.

The storm clouds had parted, and bright sunlight radiated from behind them.

Maybe it was turning out to be a nice day after all.

Chapter 12

I hate confrontations.

A few of my pastor friends seem to live for the moments they can take on troublemakers in their churches. That's never been my style. In my opinion, my clergy friends have often been too confrontational for their own good. I know at least two who have lost their positions because of it. On the other hand, I suppose they would respond that I'm too nonconfrontational for my own good.

Maybe they're right.

I can think of quite a few times over my fifteen years at Incarnation when I had remained silent when I should have spoken up. Partly this has to do with how I was mentored. I worked as a youth pastor for a few years before I took on my first senior pastorate. The pastor I worked under told me to choose my battles carefully and not to be too quick to jump in when there was a conflict in the church.

His sound wisdom played again in my ears. "Most of those little skirmishes will resolve themselves if you give them enough time. But once the senior pastor steps in, it instantly becomes a big deal."

I liked his advice, particularly because it fit my personality perfectly. I've always had a condition I refer to as "confrontational brain freeze." Whenever I need to get serious with someone about a problem or conflict, my mind locks up. I don't know what to say or how to say it. It's as though these things always catch me by surprise. Most of the time, I just stand around looking and feeling stupid. So, avoiding face-to-face confrontations comes naturally to me.

Ironically, my reluctance to confront others has helped me on a few occasions by keeping me from saying something I would later regret. But those times have been few and far between. Mostly it just means that I avoid dealing with minor problems until they have become major.

But no matter how I looked at it, the situation I faced with Clifton Stoner and some currently unnamed members of the church board was anything but a minor problem. Clifton and his cronies were on the move. I had to decide if I would be proactive, which would involve facing Clifton directly, or reactive, which meant waiting until he dropped whatever bomb was in the works.

I sat at my desk, holding my cell phone in my hand. I had Clifton's number programmed into my speed dial. I knew I should just call him and get it over with. Better the devil you know than the devil you don't.

With a sigh, I laid down the phone. I couldn't do it.

My rationalization was that I was acting out of loyalty to Flora. If I called her husband, he would know she had been talking to me. I told myself that I couldn't betray her confidence.

That was bogus, of course. The very reason she'd come to see me was so that I could try to head off, or at least be prepared for, whatever Clifton and the others were planning.

There was no reason to kid myself any longer. I just didn't have the stomach for conflict. When I saw it coming, I ran the other way. Like a soldier going AWOL at the first signs of a battle, I didn't wait for the first gunshot. I headed for the hills as soon as I heard the rumble of enemy tanks.

Face it—I'm a coward.

A light went on in my mind. Call it an epiphany; call it whatever you want. In that instant, I made a life-changing decision. And I knew exactly with whom I needed to talk.

"You're doing what?" Philip Treadway set his coffee cup down and gave me an incredulous look.

"I'm resigning. I've had enough of pastoral ministry."

"I don't believe it."

"Believe it. I'm done."

He raised an eyebrow, looking at me as if I had lost my mind. "What brought this on?"

I shrugged. "A lot of things. Mostly, I just finally realized that I must not be suited for this job."

"'A lot of things' doesn't tell me anything. What? Did you just wake up today and decide you didn't want to be a preacher anymore?"

I shifted uncomfortably on the stool. "Clifton."

Now Philip's expression changed from disbelief to disdain. "Really? You're letting that guy scare you away from doing what you love? Come on, bro. I thought I knew you better than that."

"It's complicated. And it's not just Clifton."

"So what is it?"

My throat tightened. I had run these thoughts through my head but never voiced them. I took a deep breath, trying to keep my emotions under control. "I don't have what it takes."

Philip tilted his head a bit, almost as if he hadn't heard me. But I knew he had. Then his expression changed again, this time from disdain to concern. "You're *serious*."

It wasn't a question.

"I've never been more serious in my life."

Philip studied his coffee cup for a long moment, and

then he looked back up at me. "You know I've always been straight with you."

I nodded. "That's what I like most about you."

"And you know I don't have much use for God or church."

I nodded again.

"So you understand that I don't have an agenda when I tell you that I think you're making a huge mistake."

That statement caught me somewhat by surprise. I honestly hoped he would say something like, "It's about time."

"Why do you say that?" I asked.

Philip took the carafe off its warming plate and refilled our cups. "I've known a lot of preachers in my day, and I wouldn't give two cents for the lot. But you're the exception. I've known you for fifteen years, and I've watched you. You practice what you preach. For you to quit would be a great loss."

The faint sound of a siren broke into our conversation. It was enough of an interruption to allow me to rein in my emotions. I cleared my throat and took a sip of coffee.

"Thanks. That means a lot, coming from you."

"I mean every word of it. You know I'm not someone who thinks all the evil in the world can be traced to religion. I have my own problems with God, but I don't begrudge others the right to believe. Those people need good leaders.

You're one of the few good Christian leaders I've ever met."

I smiled. "I appreciate that."

"You don't really plan to quit, do you?"

I took another swallow of coffee. "I can't do it anymore. No matter what I try to do, I run into a brick wall."

"So get another church."

"Easier said than done."

"Better yet, start your own church."

I raised my eyebrows. "Would you come?"

A wry smile creased his face. "You wouldn't want me in your church."

The sound of the siren grew louder. We both looked toward the storefront just as an ambulance blew by on the interstate. I said a silent prayer for whatever the situation was then drained my coffee cup.

Philip reached for the carafe. I waved him off. "That's enough for me. Too much caffeine today."

Philip repeated his question. "So what about starting a new church?"

I shook my head. "It wouldn't do any good. It would just be the same problem with different people. I don't have the stomach for all the politics and infighting."

"But if you start your own church, you can. . ."

Before Philip could finish his sentence, two more sirens interrupted him. Seconds later a Georgia state trooper's cruiser raced past the lumberyard, followed by another ambulance.

"Something's up." My body stiffened, and I focused more clearly on the street outside.

"Accident." Philip shrugged. "Happens all too often. I don't suppose a week goes by that I don't see the police and EMTs flying by my front window."

I was about to reply when I heard a fourth siren, and then a fifth. On the heels of those sounds, two more ambulances sped past the window.

"If it's an accident," I said, "it's a big one."

A look of sadness etched Philip's face. "I hope nobody was killed."

We moved closer forward and watched out the front window.

"Anyway," Philip continued after a moment, "if you were to start your own church, you could establish the ground rules. I heard what you said at Otis's funeral. What you said about incarnating Jesus is one of the most sensible things I've ever heard a preacher say. If you really believe that, you could start a church and make that your basic principle—incarnating Jesus to the world. People who weren't interested could go somewhere else."

"It might start out that way, but sooner or later it would end up the same as any other church."

"How do you know that?"

I grinned and shook my head. "You, a guy who has given up on God, are asking me why I believe another church is not the answer?"

"Okay, okay." He held up his hands. "I just hate to see you like this. And I'm worried about you. If you quit being a pastor, what will you do?"

"I haven't thought that far ahead."

The wail of sirens filled the air. It seemed as though every emergency vehicle in Belvedere and the surrounding area was responding to something. Philip and I exchanged worried glances. A second later, my cell phone rang. Caller ID identified the caller as Jayne.

"Hi there. What's up?" Immediately, I felt a sinking feeling in the pit of my stomach.

Her sobs blasted into my ears and then jammed into my heart. She fought for control and after several seconds was able to share her news with me. I listened wordlessly, feeling as if my whole body had gone numb. My throat constricted, but somehow I managed to reply. "I'll get over there right away. Can you take the truck and pick up Hannah?"

Philip watched me intently. When I hung up, I could feel tears brimming in my eyes.

"There's been a shooting at the high school."

Chapter 13

No, no, no, no, no!

The words clamored in my head like rocks banging inside a metal trash can as I blew through stop signs and traffic signals on my way to the school. Jayne gave me no details because she had none to give. A church member whose husband was a police officer called her and told her there had been a shooting. But that was all she knew.

As I rushed toward the school, I blinked tears away and tried to pray, but the best I could manage was a weak, "Please, God. No." I couldn't formulate the words or the thought because it was unthinkable. The unspoken prayer of my heart bounced in my brain, *God, not Brandon. Please, not Brandon.*

I knew that hundreds of other parents prayed the same prayer right now, but at the moment I didn't care about them. My only thoughts were for my son.

As I drove, the arguments Brandon and I had

exchanged flowed through my mind in an unbroken loop. I remembered every word he said, every word I had said. I hated the tension between us, and right now it didn't matter who was right or wrong. Would it have been different if Brandon and I hadn't been fighting over the last few days? I didn't know, and at the moment, I didn't care. I only wanted to be able to hug my boy and tell him I loved him.

My iPhone rang. The call was from Jenny Stewart, mother of Charlene, a teen girl in our church.

I picked up. "Hi, Jenny."

At first, all I heard was sobbing on the line.

"Jenny?"

She managed to get out a question through her sobs. "Have you heard?"

"Yes, I'm on my way to the school now. Is Charlene okay?"

It took her a few seconds to gain her composure. "I don't know yet. I'm outside the school, but they won't let us get close. Kids are coming out of the building, but I can't see her anywhere." Her voice became shrill as panic set in. "What am I going to do?" More sobs.

"Take a deep breath and try to relax. Where are you?"

"On the southeast corner of Hickory Street and Avery Creek Way."

"Okay, hang on. I'll be there in just a few minutes."

When I was five blocks away from the school, traffic

snarled. Cars and trucks, many probably driven by worried parents and relatives, clogged the road and brought traffic to a standstill.

I swung into a shopping center parking lot, grabbed my keys, and started running. I wasn't the only one on foot. People ditched their cars wherever they could find space— even in the driveways and yards of complete strangers. The closer I got to the school, the bigger the running throng became. Ahead of me, I saw a few people I recognized, but no one from my congregation. Incarnation didn't have a lot of young people. Then I rounded the corner as the campus came into view.

It was like a scene from a disaster movie—only terribly real.

It looked as though every emergency vehicle within a two-hundred-mile radius had responded. A sea of police cruisers, SWAT vans, fire trucks, and ambulances—all with lights flashing—filled the streets surrounding the school. Law enforcement had already set up a perimeter. The Belvedere Police Department's newly purchased mobile command center stood at the center of the activity, while patrol cars blocked the road and officers stood guard to prevent access to the school building.

Hundreds of people crowded around the perimeter set up by the police. Some were yelling, others crying. From a distance, the mass of people looked like fans trying to get into a rock concert or into shops on Black Friday. The crowd pressed the limits, and as I got closer, the sound of weeping grew louder.

I glanced beyond the crowd to the school building and saw several large groups of students run out the front doors and toward the waiting crowd. Some got to the far side of the crime scene tape and collapsed as they sobbed. Others walked arm in arm as they clutched each other for support. Parents and students scanned each other, looking for familiar faces. Sons, daughters, mothers, fathers, siblings. When a connection was made, a face recognized, tearful reunions followed. Teenagers who a few hours earlier would have been embarrassed to be seen hugging their parents, now eagerly embraced them and poured out their grief and shock as if they were small children.

As heartbreaking as the scene of the family reunions was, there was a worse scene there. As students and teachers continued to flood out of the building, some of the parents anxiously searched for their children in the throng. They shouted out their names in hope that somewhere in the mass of people, their son or daughter would be safe and sound. As time passed and they didn't find their loved ones, the pitch and intensity of their screams intensified.

EMTs burst out of one side door, wheeling a gurney

with a boy on it. A ventilation bag covered his mouth and a young woman squeezed the bag as they rushed toward one of the waiting ambulances. They moved too fast for me to get a look at the boy's face.

I made my way to the corner of Hickory and Avery Creek, looking for Jenny Stewart.

As I came upon the crowd, I, too, began to call out the name of my child. "Brandon!"

Students still streamed out of the school. I looked at every one of them, hoping to see my son. From this distance it was difficult to make out faces, so I judged by hair color and body type. Brandon had blond hair and a slight build. That was part of the problem. He didn't stand out in a crowd.

I pressed into the mass of people as I scanned for heads and faces. I couldn't see Brandon anywhere. Every time a new cluster of teenagers fled the building, I looked for him. All I saw were teenagers with terrified expressions of horror and grief.

As each group of students cleared the building and made their way toward the waiting crowd, spontaneous reunions broke out. Parents who found their children embraced. Kids who had been holding their emotions inside collapsed into waiting arms. Teens who hadn't yet found family members gathered and hugged, sobbing.

That was when I finally saw Jenny Stewart. She'd

worked her way to the front of the crowd so she could get a better view. Charlene had just come from the school building, and they were tearfully embracing.

I felt my phone vibrate. Jayne.

I could barely hear her voice above the din, but even so I noticed the tension, the fear in her tone. She had a question but was almost afraid to ask it.

"Is Brandon all right?"

My throat felt thick. I couldn't get the words out.

Jayne misread my pause. "Oh no! Please, God, no!"

"It's not that," I said quickly. "I just haven't been able to find him yet."

It was a comfort but only a small one. For all we knew right then, Brandon might well be lying dead in the school.

Determination replaced fear in her voice. "I'm coming over there."

Considering the situation, I needed to be firm. "No. Hannah doesn't need to see this."

As the minutes passed, fewer and fewer students came out of the school. What was at first a rush now slowed to a trickle. Reunions were fewer, and the sounds coming from the crowd subsided. Parents and teens who had found each other began to drift away from the school. A dread hush fell on those of us who had not yet found our children.

Jenny and Charlene stood about a hundred feet away.

I walked toward them, hoping to ask Charlene what had happened. Had she seen Brandon? But before I could get over there, a police officer whisked them away.

That was when I saw Clifton Stoner.

He stood by himself near an ambulance. He looked lost and bewildered.

Flora!

In my concern over Brandon, I hadn't thought about Flora Stoner's volunteer work for the school. I pushed through the milling crowd and made my way over to Clifton.

He saw me coming, but it was as if he didn't recognize me. His gaze looked blank, empty.

"Clifton," I called as I drew near.

He looked at me with red-rimmed eyes, still appearing as though he were trying to process the scene before him.

I called his name a second time.

He started, as if pulled from a trance. His eyes filled with tears, but he blinked them back.

"Is Flora all right?"

Clifton's chin quivered, and he looked down. An almost imperceptible shake of his head told me all I needed to know.

He spoke softly. "She's still in there."

"What happened?"

He pulled a linen handkerchief from his coat pocket

and wiped his eyes. "They haven't told me anything."

"How do you know she's still in there, then?"

"One of the teachers told me."

When Clifton looked at me again, his face was etched with pain. "What am I going to do without her, Steve?"

I looked into his anguished eyes and wanted to offer some comfort for him, but I was tongue-tied. In this moment, the standard answers felt like empty platitudes. I wasn't about to quote the old standby from Romans 8:28, "All things work together for good to those who love God." That never fits a situation like this one.

In my heart, I believed that no matter what happened, God would somehow bring good from it. But right then, as I still awaited news about Brandon, I felt nothing but pain and uncertainty.

Before I could offer even a lame answer to Clifton's question, a police officer with a bullhorn called for our attention.

"The school has been evacuated. We have a list of students and teachers who have been taken to area hospitals. Officers are posting copies of it around the perimeter."

I saw a Belvedere police officer with a staple gun tack a list to a tree about twenty feet away. The tree was almost instantly surrounded by people as each tried to get a look at the names.

Chapter 14

Three students had been killed and seven injured. The shooter, a sixteen-year-old named Tyler Wooten, had turned the gun on himself and lay in a coma at Belvedere Hospital. One adult, a school volunteer who had successfully shielded several students, had been killed: *Flora Stoner*.

Immediately, I was faced with two monumental challenges—coping with Brandon and the trauma he was under from the experiences of the day and the loss of Flora Stoner. Dealing with Brandon would be especially difficult because of the wall that stood between us. And Flora's death affected me in a multitude of ways. How could I reach Clifton in his grief, considering his animosity toward me? How would a second major death in the congregation in such a short period of time affect us all? I had to plan the memorial service to celebrate Flora's life. But what loomed in front of me perhaps most of all was the personal loss of my staunchest supporter at a critical time in the life of the congregation.

Prayer was the answer, and a heartfelt prayer it was. "Lord, help! I need You now as never before."

I finally spotted Brandon as he and several of his classmates straggled out of the school. In wonderment, they glanced around at what they had not expected to see—police and other officials all over the place but very few students and parents. Almost everyone but those who had been called to deal with the crisis had already gone.

As I ran to Brandon and tried to give him a hug, he became stiff as a board. It was like trying to hug a tree. He quickly pulled away. Was it because of his feelings toward me, or was he embarrassed by my display of affection? Earlier, virtually all of the parents and students eagerly accepted hugs from one another. Was it the circumstances that had changed or that the relationship between my son and me had not changed?

As we wove our way through the maze of vehicles still on the scene and headed toward our minivan a couple of blocks away, I felt as if I was trudging through an unreal world rather than a town I knew so well. How could this have happened in Belvedere, of all places? What was the world coming to?

Looking over at Brandon, I could see that he also was trying to cope with this new reality. He walked with his head down, shaking it in disbelief from time to time. I didn't try to say anything to him but instead grumbled what I hoped were manly, comforting sounds. Once we were in the minivan, I asked, "Do you want to talk about it?"

He simply shook his head.

Back at the house, the scene was emotional. Both Jayne and Hannah, tears in their eyes, ran out to hug Brandon, and he seemed to accept freely their attention. Never had I felt so inadequate to deal with a situation as I did now. Feeling weak in the knees and weaker in the brain, I shepherded my little family into the house and got them seated around the living room, despite Brandon's apparent preference to go to his bedroom. The easy way out was to deal with the situation later. Instead, I steeled myself with a determined look and said, "We need to talk about this."

Brandon sat on the edge of his chair, looking ready to launch himself out of the room at the first opportunity. He didn't make eye contact with anyone. Jayne wrung her hands and constantly glanced around, as if to try to read the minds of the children. Hannah held Skeeter in her lap in what looked like a desperate grip, needing the love and assurance of the little dog.

I leaned forward, my hands gripped together to keep from jumping up and bear-hugging Brandon. "Son, we were *so* worried."

As if reading my mind but placing an unfair inference

to it, he jumped up, fists clenched. "It's not my fault that we were hung up in there so long!"

"I didn't mean that it was your fault. It's just that we love you. Your mom and I were afraid you had been injured. And then, when all of the other kids came out and you didn't, I was frankly terrified."

Reluctantly, Brandon settled back down and began to tell us what had happened.

"I don't know how, but when we first heard the shooting, Mr. Crawford seemed to know that something bad was happening and we needed to get to a safe place. He rushed us—the whole class—into a room where they keep school supplies and got us crammed in there. We waited in there for what seemed forever, long after the shooting had ended. By the time he let us out, everyone else but the cops had cleared the building."

Jayne let out a deep, shaky breath. "Thank God for Mr. Crawford."

We all breathed a collective sigh of relief along with her. Yet Brandon appeared wired—fidgety and perplexed— while Hannah seemed to be bursting with unanswered questions. Was now the time to talk more about the situation? Surely it was. In a sense, this was the most traumatic thing that had happened in our life together as a family. We needed to process as much of it as we could while it was still so glaringly before us. Where to start?

"Son, did you know this boy who did the shooting?"

The answer had to be drawn out of Brandon. He clearly didn't want to talk about the matter, but it was my judgment that it would be better if he did.

"Naw," he replied. "Mr. Crawford said his name is Tyler Wooten. I saw him around some, but he's a year or so older than me, so we didn't have any classes together. He seemed like a loner; never saw him with other guys around him."

A shockwave went through my body as I realized I knew the shooter's mother. I'd had a nice conversation with her a couple of years ago. Not an appropriate time for me to bring that into the discussion!

In response to Brandon's comment, I nodded. "I guess that's often the case with people who end up committing horrendous acts. They feel alone, that no one cares about them, and life becomes more than they can bear. It's sort of a self-fulfilling prophecy—the more they feel that way, the more it becomes true because they drive everyone else off."

Hannah had a puzzled look on her face. "Was that what happened to Mr. Otis?"

"No, honey. Mr. Otis felt lonely, but he knew people cared for him. He would never have done something to hurt others."

Brandon dropped back against his chair. "But Dad, how

could this guy have done what he did?"

My heart leaped at Brandon's question. It was the first time he had shown any interest in what I thought about anything for too long.

"It's going to take some time to figure that one out, son. We can't really know what's going on with a person until we can get into their head and their life. As I said, being a loner is probably one part of the picture. What was his home life like? What resentments might he have had? Why did he have no faith, no sense of responsibility to others, no hope for the future? Those are some of the things that might tell us why he would do something like this."

I hoped that my answer would help Brandon take a look at his own life. I reminded myself that the teenage years are stressful—a time of transition between childhood and maturity and finding out who you really are. I could see Brandon fighting his way through this quest for identity. And of course I didn't particularly like the way he was doing it.

"Were a lot of people killed?" was suddenly Hannah's wide-eyed question.

Jayne put her arm around our daughter. "Sweetheart, a few were killed and some others were hurt." She had more details than I did because the phone lines had been busy. "One terrible thing," she continued, "is that Mrs. Stoner was one of the ones killed."

"*Our* Mrs. Stoner?" was Hannah's horrified response. Flora Stoner was not only a key figure in the church but a close friend of the family. To Hannah, Mrs. Stoner appeared indestructible. For her to have been killed seemed impossible. She immediately broke down in tears.

In the meantime, Brandon slumped in his chair, head down and continually pulling his left foot over the carpet as though trying to smooth it down. Nervous tension. Pondering. I had no idea what might be going on in his mind. I wasn't all that sure what was going on in mine!

"It's really important that both of you let us know how you are feeling and what you are thinking over the coming days. Brandon, what's happened has been a tough deal. You may have lost friends, or they may be in the hospital. Everybody's in shock. I know I haven't been the father you want me to be for quite a while, and it has been a problem between us. Please, let's put that aside. I love you and want to be the father you need. Let me know what you're feeling and how I can help."

Brandon made no verbal response, just sat with his head bent and closed his eyes.

"Okay?"

"Okay, I guess," he mumbled. I decided not to pursue it.

I hoped the children had absorbed what we had told

them. But deep down, I knew they were a long way from understanding what had happened, and Brandon was a long way from his personal need for healing. Jayne and I would have to be very loving and understanding of the children over the coming weeks and ready to talk and counsel them as needed.

As I sat thinking about that when Jayne and I were alone, she, as always, read my thoughts. "The problem is, you two are too much alike."

I turned on her, my face mirroring my frustration. "What do you mean?"

"You and Brandon. You're both hardheaded, and you keep too much to yourselves. And neither of you likes confrontation. So you stuff things down. One of you is going to have to change. . .at least in your attitude toward the other. And guess what? It has to be you." She poked me in the chest. "He's still just a kid. He's not going to figure this out. You're the adult. If you truly want a breakthrough with him, and I know you do, you're the one who has to figure out how to do it."

I swallowed hard. I didn't like the truth of what Jayne had said.

"Any suggestions?" I threw out as a trial balloon.

She thought for a while. With a sigh, she broke the silence. "Maybe you should share with him what you're going through rather than always trying to guess what he is thinking and then getting nowhere. You're carrying a load right now, buster, and it affects all the rest of us. Brandon may still be a child in most respects, but he is growing into a young man in other ways. He needs to start dealing with the real world rather than escaping into video games. You are the best one to help him take that step by sharing with him the decisions you face. It may scare the heck out of him for you to do so, but it could help him grow up."

Lord, I know why You blessed me with this woman, I said silently.

I kissed her on the cheek. "Thanks. I'll give it a try."

Chapter 15

Dealing with Brandon was one thing; dealing with Clifton Stoner was something else altogether.

I drove to Clifton's house as soon as things had calmed down in our own. The Stoner home was one of the finest in Belvedere. Situated on a large and well-landscaped piece of land, white columns across the front, it was an imposing structure. Already a number of cars lined the ample parking area around the house, and I knew the owners of most of them.

I was greeted at the door by Clifton's daughter Carolyn, who, with her husband and children, lived in Belvedere and were members of Incarnation Church. Carolyn's grief reflected in her red eyes as the signs of pain and disbelief etched along the frown lines on her face. She greeted me courteously and ushered me into the large living room, twice as long as wide, with big windows, an imposing fireplace, and enough chairs and couches to accommodate a crowd as large as the one gathered there that day. Most of the family and close friends were already present.

My arrival was acknowledged by nods and a few hand-shakes, but they seemed somewhat perfunctory. Maybe it was the grief and solemnity of the situation, or maybe I was becoming paranoid about where I stood as pastor of Incarnation Church. In any event, being clergy in such a situation has its advantages. Instead of being forced to stand around and make awkward small talk, a pathway was cleared for me to go directly to Clifton.

Carolyn led me to where Clifton sat on the couch with his head in his hands. I knelt in front of him. "Clifton, we are all devastated. You and your family have lost one of the finest people I've ever known. She was, you know, like fam-ily to us as well. We are all here for you to serve in this sit-uation in any way we can. Jayne would have come with me, but she's trying to help Brandon and Hannah sort through all of this. It has probably been the most traumatic day in the history of Belvedere."

Stoner took my hand and through sobs thanked me for being there. Here was this man of wealth, power, and prominence crying like a baby. I could no longer hold back my emotions and soon sobbed with him. We weren't the only ones in tears among the family and friends who were gathered around the large room.

What would be the impact of the loss of this great

woman on our little community? She had mothered all of us in one way or another. The magnitude of Flora's loss and the evidence of the great affection for her poured out in profound grief around the room. The rest of us would survive, but what about Clifton?

And how would he deal with the injustice of it all? In helping out at the high school, Flora had been doing something she didn't need to do. She simply loved being around children. She loved helping others, and as a former teacher, that was where she felt she wanted to be. Standing against the shooter to protect the children was also what would have been expected of this special woman, and yet what a waste! I knew people asked themselves, *How could God let this happen?*

I sort of wondered that myself. But I was the one who had to preach a sermon of faith at her memorial service. I knew I would work it through. God's ways are far beyond our capacity to understand them, and certainly God did not intend Flora to be killed. People have free will and bad things can happen to good people as a result. But still. . .

I put my arm on Clifton's back, shook his hand again, and said what comforting words I could. It was time for me to move on and let others come to him.

Arrangements for the memorial service and dealing with the many other matters that follow sudden death would come later. For now the important thing was that Clifton Stoner was able to express his grief and to know that he was supported by family and friends who loved Flora and cared for him. For me it was a relief to know that Stoner seemed to bid me no ill will in connection with church matters—at least for now.

I took time to talk with members of the family, assuring them that the memorial service for Flora would meet their expectations. We always did that sort of thing well at Incarnation Church. I was confident that this would be no exception; but then, it seemed to be a season of surprises.

Chapter 16

Events were unfolding at breakneck speed. As soon as I got home from the Stoner house, Jayne told me that the principal at the high school, Amanda Cook, had called. She was a member of Incarnation Church. Apparently she wanted me to go to the hospital to help Tyler Wooten's mother, who coped with two major tragedies: the horrible thing her son had done and what seemed to be his impending death from a self-inflicted gunshot wound.

I should, of course, have seen the danger in this new situation more clearly than I did. Politically speaking, it was a trap, though that was certainly not what Mrs. Cook, the good-hearted person that she was, intended. She knew Mrs. Wooten needed help, and her immediate reaction was to call on someone to provide it.

If I had thought it through, I would have realized that helping Mrs. Wooten could make me very unpopular with the people in Belvedere who might hold resentments against her because of what her son had done. They would feel that she needed no help, and providing it to her was some sort of sacrilege.

As much as I hate to admit it, my own pride probably caused me to fail to assess the situation from the start. In view of my current misgivings about my position at Incarnation, it made me feel good that Mrs. Cook immediately thought of me as the one to help Mrs. Wooten. In retrospect I realized she may have tried to get help from other ministers first. In any event, I was the one who said yes, setting myself up for a whole new bundle of grief.

I actually had once met Connie Wooten, a maid who cleaned rooms at the motel. It was strictly by chance. The Belvedere Ministerial Association, a couple of years earlier, had inaugurated something called Operation Christmas Basket. The idea was for the pastors to deliver baskets of food at Christmastime to those who lived in the poorer areas of town. It would give us an opportunity not only to do something thoughtful for others in need, but it would let them know that they were welcome to attend our church. I was assigned to make my deliveries at the trailer park where Mrs. Wooten lived.

In retrospect, I'm not sure it was a very good idea. Most of the people I called on that day seemed to resent the gesture. It was probably pride on their part that made it hard to accept the gift. But that was not the case with Connie

Wooten. Her trailer was near the front of the park, so she was the first one I called on. She really appreciated the basket, and we had a nice visit. When I invited her to attend Incarnation Church and left her with a brochure, she was polite but gave me a "it'll never happen" look. But all in all, my memories of Mrs. Wooten were pleasant ones.

Once I made the decision to go see her, the other questions began to pop into my brain. Why did I have to be the one to go see about her? Didn't I have enough on my plate—dealing with Flora's death, the problems I seemed to have created at church by my incarnation challenge, whether I should resign and go elsewhere, and how to break through the wall that existed between our son and myself?

I, frankly, felt sorry for myself. I also felt overwhelmed. As I threw that "Why me?" question into the air, I got the unwelcomed answer I should have expected: *"As the Father has sent Me, I also send you."*

I remembered the story I had heard while training to be a pastor in seminary about an early follower of Christ who felt she was doing the best she could but was overwhelmed. As she traveled in the back of a horse cart to get where she believed the Lord wanted her to go, it hit a large boulder and bounced her off onto the road. As she stood and dusted herself off, her response was, "Lord, when You do things like this to Your friends, it's no wonder You have so few of them!"

I symbolically dusted myself off and headed to the hospital.

Belvedere Hospital is more than adequate for a small town, and the medicinal smells and bright corridors are typical of big-city facilities. I knew my way to the intensive care unit, where Tyler Wooten lay in a coma. As I arrived, his mother stood in the hallway wringing her hands.

Connie Wooten was probably in her forties, plain in appearance, thin, and with the countenance of someone who was overworked, overwrought, and perpetually tired. We found a waiting room nearby that was fortunately empty of other people.

She recognized me, and we went through the formalities of "good to see you again" even though we did so almost through gritted teeth because of the weight each of us was feeling.

I helped her get seated in the functional, chair-lined room and pulled another chair close enough to hear her clearly without forcing her to talk above a low, conversational tone.

As I sat there with her, Mrs. Wooten seemed totally lost. The hollow look in her eyes said it all. *What has happened, and what am I to do about it?* Her body trembled and her hands clutched a well-used tissue in her lap. I didn't know if she was going to be able to tell me her needs or just collapse in a pile of grief.

I tried to give her a sympathetic look, because sympathy was definitely what she needed, but I wasn't comfortable in physically reaching out to this person I had only seen once before. I felt like a guy who approached a girl at a dance and then wasn't sure he wanted to dance with her. It felt awkward.

Fortunately, she broke the ice. "I'm glad you've come, Mr. Long, but I don't know what to say to you."

"First things first, Mrs. Wooten. How is your son?"

"The doctors say he is in a coma, and I know they don't expect him to live. What am I going to do? I don't want him to die, but it would almost be worse for him if he lives."

"Well, let's cross that bridge when we come to it." I leaned close, my hands folded in front of me. "I know it's painful for you, but can you tell me how all of this could have happened?"

Connie Wooten shook her head in disbelief of it all. I waited as she took some time to gather herself, and then she began with a sigh. "Tyler worshiped his dad. They were like best pals. Lou, my husband, was an auto mechanic, and he and Tyler loved to work on machines and equipment of any kind. And they loved to hunt. Lou taught Tyler about guns."

Guns! She suddenly gulped, her hand to her mouth and

her eyes wide. Fresh tears swam in them, and she appeared to have a hard time continuing her train of thought.

"Take your time." I kept my voice steady and reassuring. "I know this is hard, but if I'm going to be of any help, I need to know as much as you are willing to tell me."

After a long pause, Connie continued. "Anyway, like I said, Tyler loved his father. Then Lou got cancer and died two years ago."

Again, Mrs. Wooten's words brought on another flow of emotions as she realized she was on the verge of losing the rest of her little family, her whole world.

After more tears, another pause, and then visibly trembling, she continued. "I don't know. It's as though Tyler blamed his dad for getting sick and dying. . .like Lou had abandoned him. He handled his pain in a strange way. Instead of grieving, he just got mad. At his father for leaving him, at me because I wasn't able to fill the gap, and at the world in general. And it wasn't just for a little while. Over the last two years, it's as though his resentment has grown.

"There've been other things, too, of course. With Lou and me both working, we made enough to get by. But now we have to live hand to mouth, food stamps and all that. Lou hadn't put much aside, and what little there was—and more—got wiped out with his illness. So I'm sure Tyler resented not having things the other kids have, not being able to dress as nice as they do.

"That and us living in a trailer park and his mother working as nothing more than a maid at the motel. I'm sure the other kids at school were ugly to him, and the more his resentment showed, they probably treated him even worse."

In addition to pain, shame oozed into the picture. She continued to wring her hands. She would gaze down and sigh hopelessly and then look up at me, wide-eyed, like a puppy begging for a treat. She seemed so genuine and vulnerable, and her words tore at my heart.

"You're really helping me get the picture. I realize this is hard for you, but you're telling me the sort of things I need to know if I can be of any help." *That is, if I can help her.*

In truth, I had no idea how I could be of help, and I felt a little guilty for intruding so deeply into her privacy and her feelings. But I knew from many years of counseling that she was sharing vital information. So I encouraged her to keep going.

Again the sigh, the downcast look. "So," she continued, "he's become a loner. Not doing well in school, not showing any interest in sports or girls. Just keeping his head buried in that silly PlayStation playing games that aren't good for him and cleaning those guns his father left him."

At this point, Mrs. Wooten broke down completely, dissolving into tears.

My heart truly bled for this woman. I couldn't conceive the depth of her grief, confusion, and loneliness. I reached out and took her hands in mine. I had been a pastor long enough to know that my words would be inadequate at this point. The important thing was for her not to feel alone, that someone cared for her and what she was going through. And despite my initial reluctance to get involved, I now really did care for her.

She eventually emerged from her grief long enough to say, "I just couldn't reach him. The harder I tried, the further he pulled away. And now, here we are. . . ."

I grimaced at her words because they reminded me of my concerns about my own son. I told myself to put that on hold. I had my hands full helping Connie Wooten.

Long ago I learned how difficult it is to console someone who has no background of faith, and that certainly seemed to be the case with Connie Wooten. The first step was simply to be a friend who cares.

"Mrs. Wooten. . ."

"Please call me Connie, Mr. Long."

Big step! I took a deep breath. She had just leaped across the divide between acquaintances and friends by asking me to call her by her first name. It freed me up to confront her with the faith issue.

"Connie, there is no way for me to feel what you are

going through at this time. No one can. But I can tell you that God loves you and cares very much about you and what you are dealing with. It may be impossible for you to believe that, but through the love of God, Mrs. Cook, the principal at the high school, called me to visit you, and I came. May I just sit here with you until we know something more from the doctors?"

"I know you have other things you need to be dealing with, Mr. Long. Don't feel that you need to stay with me when others need you."

The quality and sincerity of Connie Wooten came out even more clearly. Here she was, dealing with something few people, thank God, will ever have to deal with, and her concern was for me.

"Well, let's just wait and see." I gave her hand a soft squeeze.

Over the next couple of hours, we sat together in the intensive care waiting area. People would stick their heads in the door from time to time, but the doctor had yet to appear. The longer we waited, the greater the tension. Connie Wooten continued to alternate between times of crying and wild-eyed attention to what went on around her. I prayed silently and spoke words of support from time to time as seemed appropriate.

I have to admit, however, there was another thought

rattling around in my brain. It was about Brandon. Was there any similarity between Tyler Wooten and Brandon Long? One thing that linked them was their mutual fascination with games played on electronic gadgets, wasting time—as far as I was concerned—that could have been spent in interaction with others. Also, I could picture Tyler as sullen, a trait I had unfortunately noted in my son—at least in his contacts with me. Was Brandon a loner? Could he be developing the same symptoms that led Tyler to such horrendous action?

I didn't really believe it, but the thought jarred my reverie. I needed to spend more time with my son. More constructive time.

Suddenly my thoughts were interrupted by the appearance of a doctor. "I'm sorry, Mrs. Wooten. We did everything we could."

As the distraught mother broke down in tears, I took her in my arms and let her cry it out. There was no consoling her at this point. She had said earlier, and truthfully, that it would almost be worse if Tyler lived. Even if he had healed completely from shooting himself, he would have faced trial and life in prison. But now, faced with the reality of his loss, her grief was total.

Minutes that seemed like hours went by as I tried unsuccessfully to give her comforting thoughts—such as the need to try to put it all behind her and begin a new life, that God was with her in the midst of her profound grief—things of that nature that gave me something to do but were no help at all to her.

Finally, she gathered herself together as best she could.

When she had gotten control of herself sufficiently to speak, Connie Wooten asked me a question I never saw coming. "Would you be willing to have some sort of burial service for Tyler?"

I knew at that moment that my incarnation challenge had reached a new level of reality. If I was going to be Christ to Connie Wooten, my answer would have to be yes. But I knew that my yes would be a huge affront to Clifton Stoner, my congregation, and undoubtedly, the people of Belvedere.

Regardless of the consequences, I heard myself say, "Of course I will, Connie."

Chapter 17

As I drove home from the hospital, I felt like a Ping-Pong ball being bounced back and forth—physically and emotionally. What had I gotten myself involved in? Every corner I turned seemed to confront me with a new challenge. Things were totally out of control. The one person I could count on, however, to help me sort all this out and give me the support I needed at this crucial time was Jayne. Surely that would be so, I said to myself as I arrived home.

Unfortunately, it didn't work out that way. After I had told her about the meeting with Connie Wooten, Tyler's death, and my promise to perform some sort of burial service for the boy, she responded with, "Oh, Steve, surely you haven't!"

I tried to explain to her how it had happened, and how I felt it a personal confrontation from the Lord to show I was willing to accept His incarnation challenge. She seemed somewhat mollified by my explanation as she pictured the disaster that loomed before us as a result.

Some people at Incarnation Church would be concerned that I had had *any* contact with Connie Wooten, and people throughout the community would as well. Mainly Clifton Stoner would think it completely inappropriate. What business did I have getting myself involved in the problems of those who weren't members of our church? Especially a boy and his mother who were pariahs to the community. Was I just begging for trouble?

Of course not, I told myself. It was just—so it seemed to me—something that God asked me to do. Being able to explain that to others remained the challenge.

To Jayne's credit, she let me talk it through as we sat on the sofa in the family room holding hands. In the end, she gave me a forced smile and said, "I know you believe you are doing the right thing. It's just that we have to be realistic about whatever fallout it may have."

I agreed with that!

Pivoting from one crucial subject to another, as my dear wife seemed adept at doing, she continued, "Steve, Hannah's out walking Skeeter and Brandon is in his room. Maybe this is a good time for you to share with him all this stuff that's going on in your life."

"How can I do that, sweetheart? I can't even sort it out in my own mind."

"That's the point." She nodded. "Give him a chance to help you."

That didn't seem to be a good idea to me, but what did I have to lose? I knocked on Brandon's door.

"Yeah?" came the reply.

"May I come in?"

"I guess so."

When I entered the room, it was the same dark place it always seemed to be. Only the desk light was on and the blinds partially open. Maybe that helped Brandon see the images on his Xbox more clearly. He lifted his face from the screen. But of course that threw my mind back to Tyler Wooten because I could picture a similar scene that might have been in his bedroom. So, off to a bad start with my son once again.

Brandon's countenance was as dark as the room as he turned to me, arms crossed, with anything but a welcoming look. His body language conveyed his thoughts loud and clear—why are you interrupting me when I've got something better to do?

My hope had been that Jayne had worked her magic on Brandon and that he would be more open to what I had to say. From the response I got as I stood there in the doorway, I wasn't so sure. I said a silent prayer and walked into the room.

"Could I share with you some of what's going on in my life for a few minutes? They are things that could affect all of us."

Brandon gave me a "if you *have* to" look, so I dropped down onto his bed and started talking, probably giving him an overload. But let's face it, I was overloaded!

"You were in youth church Sunday morning, so you didn't hear my sermon, but maybe you have picked up some reaction or comments."

"Not really."

"Well, here's what happened. It was sort of a combination of regular Sunday worship and a memorial service for Otis. By doing the two things together, it gave me what I thought would be an opportunity to reach the congregation in a deeper way. I gave them what I think of as being an incarnation challenge."

"What's that?" He scrunched his nose as though I had uttered a dirty word.

I wanted to tell him about Charles Sheldon and his book *In His Steps* and the, "What would Jesus do?" response to it because I knew that Brandon had seen WWJD bracelets on the arms of some of his friends. And I wanted to tell him that I thought God expected more than a WWJD response from Christians. He wanted us to incarnate Christ in our time, to *be* Christ to our world. That was the challenge I had given in the sermon, but I didn't think Brandon was ready to hear that. So I gave him the abbreviated version.

"Well. . ." I shifted my position to face him. "It's a way of looking at the Christian life. . .that God wants us to be Christians in all our thoughts and actions. I challenged them to take their faith more seriously."

That sounded kind of weak to me, but it was the best I could do to explain something to Brandon at what I believed to be his present level of understanding.

"Why are you telling me this?"

"What I said was apparently something the congregation didn't want to hear. When I asked them to come into the fellowship hall after the service to talk about it, I got zero response. Now Mr. Stoner accuses me of alienating the congregation. All he seemed to get out of the sermon was that I blamed the congregation for Otis's death."

"What's *that* all about?" Brandon's face screwed up, not following my train of thought.

"Well, as part of the sermon, I mentioned the note I had gotten from Otis after his death in which he said he couldn't stand being so lonely anymore, and I raised the question of how a member of our congregation could die of loneliness. So Mr. Stoner saw the whole thing as my accusing the congregation of not having been friendlier and more caring toward Otis. And as I'm sure you know, Mr. Stoner can stir up a lot of trouble if he sets his mind to it."

Before Brandon could react to what I had said, I was suddenly reminded of the friendship that had existed between Otis and our son, of which I had been insensitive following Otis's death, and I quickly shifted gears. Instead of babbling on about things I was dealing with, shouldn't I really be trying to find out what was going on in Brandon's life? His friendship with Otis might be a pathway into what he was thinking.

"Son, I know you cared deeply about Otis. Tell me more about him."

Because I shifted gears so abruptly in my thought process, Brandon seemed caught by surprise. He looked at me as though wondering what this had to do with anything we had been discussing. Then, accepting the situation, he responded.

"Well, he was a nice old guy. I liked working with him around the church. But I guess he thought I was too young to really talk about whatever was going on in his life."

I should have followed up with, "Son, what is going on in *your* life?" but I didn't. Instead, I just started babbling again. Probably nervousness. All the while the thought paraded through my subconscious. *This is my son. Why should I be nervous when I am around him, and why can't I carry on a meaningful conversation with him? Is it him, or is it me?*

"Otis *was* a nice guy. I know he appreciated your work, because he told me so a number of times. And he was quiet by nature. But I also think that he felt inferior to other people at Incarnation. Instead of being in church to worship with us, he probably saw himself as the hired help. He didn't have the things other people have and couldn't dress as well as the rest of us. But that was no excuse on our part. We adults should have reached out to him more effectively so that he would have felt a part of us, known that he was a part of us.

"Now, because of some things I said in that sermon, Mr. Stoner and some others think I accused Incarnation folks of being high and mighty, and as a result, we are all somehow guilty of Otis killing himself."

"So what?"

"Well, they could make things hard on me. I don't know what that might be, but I wanted you to know what's going on because it could affect all of us."

Brandon got a troubled look on his face and said, "How?"

"Honestly, I don't know." I puffed through my cheeks. "Maybe there'll be talk about me. . .unpleasant talk. . .and I just wanted you to be forewarned in case you started hearing things. Some people might even leave the church and go elsewhere."

"Oh." Brandon gave me a "what was this all about, and why does it make any difference to me?" look. He sat there with his arms still crossed and glanced over at his Xbox, as if to let me know that he was ready for me to leave.

"Please have me in your prayers, Brandon. I'm going to need them if we are going to keep this ship we call Incarnation Church afloat."

"Okay," was his nonchalant reply as he turned to his Xbox and tuned me out.

Chapter 18

Tuesday, October 17

Tuesday morning as I perched on the side of the bed with my head in my hands, Jayne came in with a cup of coffee.

"What's up?"

"Just thinking about yesterday." I gave her a forced grin through my muddled brain waves. I needed to talk, and Jayne was a wonderful and sympathetic listener. I took a sip of the badly needed and perfectly blended coffee and sighed with satisfaction for that taste of stability. I patted the bed beside me, and she sat down.

"Okay, talk to me."

I poured out my thoughts. "I'm still trying to process all that happened. I woke up with the reminder that my sermon had not only fallen flat but had antagonized the congregation, and then when I took the kids to school hoping for a breakthrough with Brandon, that bombed. I got to church and had a surprise visit from Flora that left me thinking that maybe it was going to be a good day after all. There was then a visit with Philip, followed by the horrible scene at school. Then the joy of finding out Brandon was all right but the devastating news that Flora had been killed. Next the family time with Brandon and Hannah to help us all process what had happened. Then a brief time with Clifton and his family concerning Flora, followed by the trip to the hospital to help Connie Wooten deal with what was happening in her life. Then back here with you and the kids and the chance to have a talk with Brandon that fell as flat as my sermon. I can't believe all that happened in one day. It might well have been the worst day of my life. It's no wonder I feel rode hard and put up wet this morning."

Jayne rubbed my shoulder. "You do need a break but probably won't get one. What can I do?"

"You're doing it, just by loving me and understanding. I'll go to the office and handle phone calls. There'll be preliminary stuff to do to get ready for Flora's memorial service. I'm glad she wanted to be cremated. Logistically, that makes things easier for me."

"Why did she want to be cremated?" Jayne asked. Cremation was unusual for residents of Belvedere, where the more traditional norm was visitations, open caskets, and funeral services followed by graveside services.

"Well, it's interesting. We had a long talk about it a

couple of years ago. Flora had already told Clifton she wanted to be cremated, but he wanted her to explain it to me. It had to do with her personality and, I think, her faith."

Jayne crossed her legs and looked me in the eyes. "Tell me."

Her sincere smile helped me more than the sip of caffeine. "The faith part first. She knows that once a person has died, their spirit goes to be with the Lord. The body is just an empty shell. We'll have new bodies in heaven. To put it crudely, the old one just rots in the grave if it is not cremated. I think Flora felt that leaving the body around to be looked at, carried into and out of the service, carried to the cemetery, and laid in the ground put too much focus on the body rather than the spirit."

"Do you agree with that?"

"Actually I do. Maybe it's something we'll need to talk about concerning what happens to us in the end."

The seriousness of the expression on Jayne's face made it clear this was a new issue for her and one we would, indeed, need to discuss.

"But you said it was more than a faith matter with her."

"I think it was. I believe it had to do with basic humility. She didn't want her death to be made a big thing over. She didn't want people oohing and aahing over a casket, talking about how beautiful and appropriate it was and how she looked so peaceful, etc. She just wanted people to get her death over with as quickly and easily as possible."

With a look of frustration, Jane said, "But people need to process such a loss. She was such a major person in this community. Her death is an awful tragedy. We won't want to forget her and all she has meant to us."

I scratched my eyebrow. "Yeah, that's the other side of it. But it was her choice, and it does make things easier for me. I know that's a selfish thing to say, but considering everything else that's going on, I'm grateful that we can have a memorial service and a reception afterward in the fellowship hall. Without coordinating with the funeral director, educating his staff on how to maneuver the casket in our church, organizing pall bearers—and then there's the drive to the graveside. . . ." I shrugged. "Clifton and the family will choose a later time and place for the interment of the ashes."

"Okay, then what's next for you?"

"Oh, not much." I chuckled, tongue planted firmly in my cheek. "The church, the office, thinking all of this through, beginning to get ready for what lies ahead."

Chapter 19

Betty Ferguson, our church secretary, met me at the door as I arrived at Incarnation. Betty, who might be called pleasingly plump, was normally energetic and efficient and had a cheerful disposition. This morning she seemed distracted, harassed, and in the need of direction.

"Too many phone calls already this morning?" I asked.

"You betcha!" She huffed into her bangs.

"What do you need from me?"

"Here's a list. Mr. Stoner's daughter Carolyn wants you to call her about arrangements for the memorial service Thursday, and there are some other calls you'll want to answer. I'll need your guidance on the worship bulletin. Then there are the florists! We've never gotten so many calls about flowers for a funeral service. I guess you'll want me to get with the flower guild on that."

And so it went. A busy day, but one in which I hoped to give thought to the sermon.

Memorial services are a challenge. There are standard Scripture passages to use, and I have used them many times. That's not the problem. The problem is the tone of the service itself, the atmosphere appropriate to the situation. There is a lot of difference between a service for a young person who has suffered a tragic and unexpected death and one for an elderly member of the congregation who has been fighting illness for some time. In the one you have to allow for the shock of what has happened and the underlying disappointment with God that loved ones are often feeling. In the other, there is the opportunity to thank God for a life well lived. Of course in both situations the preacher wants to assure the family and friends that the person has gone on to a much better place.

Flora's death fell somewhere between those two extremes. I wanted to honor her life and her heroic death but at the same time be sensitive to questions many would have about why she was taken from us so suddenly and in such a violent way.

Unfortunately, time for working through the best way to handle my sermon was cut short by a multitude of interruptions. The phone conversations and brief visits to the office by various people connected with Flora and with the service itself were pleasant.

But with all that was going on, I began to wonder if

I was getting paranoid about my own role, perhaps because two calls and one visit came from the three people on the church's leadership board whom I believed to have responded well to my incarnation challenge even if they hadn't shown up for the session in the fellowship hall. Instead of focusing on the tragedy of the shooting and specifically on the profound shock all of us felt because of Flora Stoner's death, these people were intent on giving me assurances about what an excellent pastor they thought I was. Why were they giving me these attaboys? Did it have anything to do with what might be going on behind my back in the church, the reason for Flora's visit with me yesterday morning?

Whereas yesterday had been filled with so much action—most of it traumatic—that I could hardly catch my breath from one situation before another hit, today was a marked contrast. There were the interruptions (phone conversations and visits from members of the congregation), details to be tended to, and thoughts about the memorial service itself, but unlike yesterday, which was a day of doing, this developed into one of thinking. And I wasn't happy with my thoughts because they were selfish ones. I was frankly worried about myself and my family—our future.

Mid-October in northern Georgia is unpredictable weather-wise. Although it's fall, one day may feel like summer and the next like winter. Tuesday was an in-between day. The temperature hovered in the sixties, and it was cloudy. That pretty well matched my feelings. I felt suspended between whatever had happened and whatever was going to happen, and like the forecast, I was gloomy.

In the midst of everything else, I got a disturbing telephone call from Philip Treadway. He led into what he wanted to say by pointing out that Belvedere was no different from other towns and cities across the country. There were good-hearted people and there were mean-spirited ones. The deaths and injuries at the high school brought out the best in the best of them and the worst in the worst of them. Children from both the well-meaning families and the bitter ones had been victims.

At that point, Philip had taken a deep breath and a sigh. "Steve, all the parents are heartbroken, but some want revenge. Because they can't wreak revenge on Tyler Woo-ten, his mother is their target."

I dropped the pen I had been holding in my hand. "You've got to be kidding!"

Another sigh. "Unfortunately not. It's easy for me to pick up the mood. There are people like Mike Troutman, owner of a small moving company and father of a girl who was killed in the shooting. Mike is a guy with an appetite for troublemaking. One of Troutman's workmen, who's also a carpenter and a frequent customer, unintentionally alerted me to some of what is going on. He told me Mike's got a real mad on, blaming that Wooten woman for what happened. And Mike is apparently talking to some of the others who agree with him. There's going to be trouble."

I fell back in my chair and let out a roar. "The woman's suffered enough!"

Philip paused a moment then dropped the next bomb. "I wish that was all I had to tell you, but it's not. I'm told that Troutman had Sam Cummings at the motel fire Connie Wooten. Cummings probably resisted, but Troutman is good at threatening and then backing it up."

My head was spinning. I thanked Philip for bringing me up-to-date, but when I hung up, I headed for the sanctuary.

I had spent too much time that day wondering about what people thought about me, whether it was time for me to be considering a move, and any number of other self-focused matters. Other thoughts popped into my mind. With all that had occurred since Sunday, it was as if I had forgotten about Otis and the fact that he died of loneliness among a congregation of people who are to love their neighbor as themselves. How could that have happened on my watch? Now my anxiety shifted to Connie Wooten and what she faced. It was time to lift my concerns to God even though the sun didn't cast its rainbow reflections through the stained glass in the way that always made me feel closer to the Almighty.

When I got home, instead of sharing my concerns with Jayne and the children, I tried to just be part of the family doing those things we would normally do on a Tuesday night—that is, if anything could be defined as normal in a pastor's life.

Chapter 20

Wednesday, October 18

The following morning, the sun reappeared, and I felt I had begun to get things in perspective. I got a fairly good night's sleep, ate a healthy breakfast, and felt ready for the day. Jayne, on the other hand, seemed perplexed.

Southern women have always amazed me. In the midst of all the turmoil going on in our lives, Jayne was concerned about what to take to the reception that would be held at Incarnation Church following the memorial service for Flora Stoner. My day would involve heading to the church office to work on final preparations for the service and specifically my sermon. In the meantime, Jayne was in a dither about the reception—more particularly, about what would be expected of her in providing a carry-in dish.

"Why don't we just pick up some fried chicken?" I asked in my ignorance and lack of sensitivity. "That's what people like."

Jayne gave me that withering look that showed I, once again, just didn't get the picture. "You know I can't do that. I am, after all, the pastor's wife. I'm supposed to show some leadership here. My cousin, you know, coauthored the book that is the gold standard for food at receptions following funerals."

I wasn't sure how to respond to that, although it seemed to me we'd had this conversation more than once in the past. So I responded in obvious ignorance, "What's your plan?"

"Well, Charlotte says tomato aspic is the choice item at a funeral reception. I'm not sure I'm up to the challenge. You've got to get the gelatin balance right or the stuff ends up being too runny or too firm. You're to clip off the top of a bunch of celery. Well, how much is that? Some people like pecans in tomato aspic, but we don't have any, and I'm not sure about the pecans anyway." She finally took a breath.

With all the issues swirling around in my mind, there was something comforting about Jayne's dilemma. The world hadn't gone completely crazy if Jayne could be concerned about tomato aspic. "I know you will do your best."

I quickly decided that now was the time to get out of the house, gave her a kiss on the forehead, and headed for my truck.

The plan for the day was to work with Betty in finalizing all of the arrangements for the service on the following day, and to prepare my sermon. There were fewer phone messages and other details for me to handle than I had expected— the joy of having an intelligent and efficient secretary. But I had difficulty concentrating on the sermon. The contacts from supporters yesterday kept surfacing in my brain.

Hadn't I put all of that behind me yesterday? I had taken it to the Lord in prayer. Yet here it surfaced all over again, an unwelcome force entering my space and creating havoc within me.

Why had those three contacted me, and why were they *so* supportive? I had originally pushed to the back of my mind Clifton Stoner's displeasure with my incarnation challenge. But Flora had taken it seriously enough to come and talk with me the day she died. "Clifton and some of the board members have been talking," she had said. Then she had added, "They're planning some sort of response to the challenge you laid out in your sermon," or something like that. She urged me to stand firm. That was like Flora. She shared my concern that Otis had died of loneliness, and she welcomed the incarnation challenge because that was where she was, spiritually speaking.

Although her support had cheered me up, the fact that I might receive such a negative reaction to my challenge had caused me to wonder if my time at Incarnation Church needed to come to an end. I had actually discussed that with Philip Treadway. Then the shooting and Flora's death had put everything on hold. Now it once more crept—unwanted—back into my mind.

I had been at Incarnation for fifteen years. I thought I knew these people. I knew what I had been teaching them over those years—what I thought to be solid Scripture-based sermons, lessons about Christian love and discipleship, challenging them to take what I had been telling them out into the world around them. I thought some of them took all of that seriously. I saw faithfulness in their faces and their actions in so many instances. I really cared for these people.

Yet I also knew that, for the most part, they were financially comfortable. They lived privileged lives. They weren't dealing with the problems that faced the vast majority of people around the world. They had nice homes, ample food, and stylish clothes. Instead of serious evangelism, their idea of a church event to catch the attention of the community had once been a fashion show—an idea I quickly squelched, to the great displeasure of some of our leading women.

So, despite my best efforts, many of our people remained shallow in their faith. Instead of my incarnation challenge being a logical next step for them, it seemed to have been a bone of contention. In the depths of my being, I relived the heartbreak of no one showing up in the fellowship hall to discuss the matter —no one other than the Stoners, and the two of them diametrically opposed to each other!

Maybe it was time for a change. It might not be my decision. My challenge to the congregation had already sparked division. When it was known that I was going to have a funeral service for Tyler Wooten, the choice of what to do might not be my own. The board might make that decision for me. Clifton Stoner controlled the board, so most likely what he decided would be their decision.

I reflected on my options. Leaving a congregation after fifteen years—especially under a cloud—was not exactly a good advertisement for my future ministry. What if I tried to plant a church somewhere—where would it be and how could I afford to do it? Knowing the folks at Incarnation, they would be generous to my family and me on our departure, even if the board forced my resignation. But our savings account was small, and even a generous gift from the church wouldn't last us long.

And what could I do other than pastor a church? Go back to work for Philip Treadway in his lumberyard? That didn't sound very productive and probably wouldn't be an option anyway. He had hired me years ago only on a part-time basis to supplement my church salary in those early days. He didn't need even a part-time guy to help him now.

I couldn't come to any conclusion. These were just troubling thoughts rattling around in my brain. What I really needed to do was to work on the sermon for tomorrow—and that, eventually, I was able to do.

Chapter 21

Edward Smalley was a big man with a big voice. The father of one of the students killed in the high school shooting, he wanted some action. The way I figure it, he didn't know what kind of action was appropriate in the circumstances, but he needed some relief from the pain of his loss, and just thinking about it only made matters worse. Therefore, he called a meeting of those who had loved ones killed or injured in the shooting to talk about what to do. A construction worker and lifelong resident of Belvedere, he was well known and generally well liked.

So, I decided I better show up once I got word of the meeting from Philip Treadway. Not to voice my opinion but to test the temperature of the waters.

The meeting happened that Wednesday evening at the Belvedere Library, which often provided space for general purpose gatherings. The room was large, set up with rectangular wooden tables that would each seat six to eight people comfortably. Around the walls were pictures of people who had been important in the history of the town and scenes of Belvedere's past.

People ambled in, somber and reflective in appearance. No small talk, just nodding of heads in recognition of fellow sufferers. There were about forty people in attendance, including Clifton Stoner.

The more high-minded people were focused on how to prevent such a tragedy in the future. Others were focused on revenge.

Once everyone was seated, Smalley opened the meeting. "We're here to talk about a tragedy that never should have happened and how to prevent anything like that from ever happening again. My wife, Margie, says that a lot of that might be trying to figure out which children in our school might be so troubled that they would do such a thing as that Wooten boy did, and how to reach them. I'm sure her point of view is a good one if it's possible. But what seems more important to me is having a patrolman at the school to prevent a crazy person from shooting at others or to stop them on the spot.

"But I'm getting ahead of myself. What we really want to do is open this up for any ideas you have. It's an opportunity to talk about what's on your mind. We've all suffered greatly from what happened, and we don't want it to happen again. But while the pain of it is so fresh on our minds, we also need healing ourselves."

That got things started, and virtually everyone had something to say.

A thirtysomething woman in the back called out, "I want to say a good word for the school system in calling off school this week, not just for the high school but for all of the city schools."

Another added, "And for providing counselors for those kids and parents who need it, though that will need to be a continuing process."

Because I had been forewarned by Philip, I wasn't overly surprised when a man I assumed to be Mike Troutman jumped up and shouted, "I want to know what we're going to do about getting that Wooten woman out of Belvedere. We're not going to get any healing as long as she is around to remind us of what her kid did to kill our children and ruin our lives."

I sucked in my breath to keep from responding. *Keep cool, Steve. You're here to listen, not to get involved.*

Troutman's outburst caused immediate and mixed reactions. Some heads nodded, but the general murmur through the crowd seemed to me one of disapproval.

Edward Smalley could see that the meeting could quickly get out of hand if revenge became the main subject. He raised his arms to calm folks down. "I don't want to prevent discussion on anything here tonight, but I think we need to focus on what we can do to prevent something like this from happening again. If some of you want to discuss other things, you can do so after we've finished with the first order of business, and that—again—is to look at protection of our children in the future."

Some people were still visibly in shock, and all looked as if they were in grief. They had a lot of ideas, but they wanted something done, and they wanted it now! It took all of Smalley's leadership skills to keep them on track over the next two hours.

As is often the case in situations like this, the opinions varied widely about the most effective preventive measures. Fortunately, not much blame was placed on the school or the local police force, though some noted that it would have been good if someone had foreseen such an event long ago. But even at that, plenty of people vented their anger of one kind or another during the discussion.

Some suggested arming the teachers and getting them trained in the use of weapons, but ultimately the majority thought this unwise because it would make guns too easily available to others in the school. Deep down there was the disturbing mental image of teachers with guns.

Ultimately, there was consensus that two things should happen. The teachers and staff at the school should be trained in how to spot troubled students and how to deal with them way in advance of tragic action occurring. And the Belvedere police should always have someone on patrol at the school during school hours. To my relief, and I think to the relief of most in the room, the mood became more cordial and cohesive.

However, after these conclusions had been reached and decisions had been made about who would go to the authorities to make the demands known, the underlying hostility on the part of some of the participants surfaced. Mike Troutman shouted, "This meeting isn't over. There's still some of us that want that woman out of town." Everyone knew who "that woman" was: Connie Wooten.

I pressed my lips together. *Here we go again!*

An uproar followed. Edward Smalley, still in the leadership role, finally gained control of the meeting. "As far as I'm concerned," he said, "we've accomplished what we came here for. If there are others of you who have a different agenda, you are free to stay and hash it out. But I, for one, want nothing to do with it."

Eight men remained in the room after the others had left. I hung around in the back of the room, trying to be as inconspicuous as possible. Mike Troutman was clearly the leader of this group. The others included relatives of students who had been killed or wounded, plus Stoner, who had lost his wife, and a few others who were troublemakers by nature.

"I got Sam Cummings to fire that Wooten woman, but we don't need her kind around here." Troutman's face reddened. "The fact that she's still here will always be a reminder to us of what that boy did and that she could have prevented the tragedy if she'd have brought him up right."

"Yeah," remarked another. "In any event, she should have let someone know he was crazy if she couldn't handle him."

A third man nodded his head rapidly and looked around the room. "And she let him have all those guns."

Those were the more rational responses. Others were more vicious in their words of condemnation. They had blood lust on their minds and wanted action but had no idea what that might be.

"What do we do?" someone finally asked.

Clifton Stoner, though an acknowledged leader in the community, listened intently but said nothing. He noticed me in the back of the room but chose to ignore my presence.

Mike Troutman spoke again. "We give her fair warning. If she doesn't leave town, we'll burn her out. She just lives in one of those trashy trailers on the edge of town. I'll take the lead. I know all of you and how to get in touch with you when needed."

This seemed to satisfy the most vengeful among them,

and no one seemed to be willing to challenge Troutman and his assessment. However, there was an uneasiness that Stoner had not spoken. Troutman looked at him, and many eyes followed his gaze.

"What do you think, Mr. Stoner?"

"I think you're right about encouraging her to leave, because as long as she is here, she is a reminder of what happened. Anything more than that, count me out."

Clifton shot me a glance as he left the room. I nodded back. Now armed with more knowledge, I felt better about the sermon I had prepared.

Chapter 22

The sanctuary of Incarnation Church overflowed with flowers and people at ten o'clock in preparation for Flora Stoner's memorial service. I had never seen such a beautiful display of flowers—an outpouring of love for one of Belvedere's most beloved citizens. And where there were no flowers, there were people—standing room only. Not only were Incarnation people there in great numbers but folks from all walks of life who had been touched by this exceptional woman, including a number of high school students.

Flora's family knew the hymns she would have wanted, and there had been easy agreement about the Scriptures to be read. The focus of the service would be on Jesus' overcoming death and offering eternal life to all who accepted Him as their Lord and Savior. But the service was equally to honor the life of Flora Stoner, and there would be plenty of opportunity for that.

Under the circumstances, I believed there should be testimonials, if that was satisfactory with the family. It was. Flora's daughter Carolyn was chosen to speak for the family. Marilyn Gregory, a lifetime friend, reminisced on a life well lived. Amanda Cook, the high school principal, dealt with Flora's contribution to the community. To me, the speakers gave perfect balance to the character of this fine woman. Her life reflected that she had been a precocious child, a popular young woman, an ideal mother, and a champion of community spirit. For me she had also been an outstanding church leader.

I based my sermon on John 11:21–27, focusing on verses 25 and 26: "I am the resurrection and the life. He who believes in Me, though he may die, he shall live. And whoever lives and believes in Me shall never die." I then used Romans 8:32–39—that nothing in creation can separate us from the love of God that is in Christ Jesus—to affirm the point.

It was my usual three-point sermon. I wanted to assure those present that Flora was now in a better place—in God's presence enjoying eternal life. But I also wanted the sermon and the memorial service itself to be a tribute to a life well lived in obedience to God. And finally, I wanted people to be filled with forgiveness and not hatred toward the boy who had committed this heinous act.

I used the Scriptures to demonstrate that this service was not meant to be a somber focus on the loss of a person so greatly loved as Flora. It was a resurrection service in which people could rejoice in what Christ has done for us in assuring us of eternal life, knowing that Flora was now praising God and growing from strength to strength in His greater presence.

Then I talked about Flora's life and what it meant to so many people. But I also focused on the nature of her death. Just as in life she had given of herself for the benefit of others, so had she done in her death. Just as Jesus Christ had innocently died for our sins, Flora had given her life protecting others who were in danger. She had been Christ to those in need and, like Jesus, had died in doing so.

I concluded with a plea for healing instead of retribution. "At times we Christians, as the body of Christ here on earth, are called upon to absorb events that evil produces. Tyler Wooten was not evil, but his actions were. . .horrible and senseless. The evil one made use of them to kill and destroy, just as he did on Good Friday. Jesus was present both times. He and Flora were called to overcome evil with good, and it cost both of them their lives. Let's not dishonor Flora or disobey God by choosing hatred and vengeance. Jesus had no clearer message than that we Christians are to be forgivers. Let forgiveness reign in your hearts, and leave the rest to God."

Following hymns and prayers, I invited people to the altar for personal prayers and had a team of leaders available to pray with those who came forward. An overwhelming number of people did, including some who were not members of Incarnation Church, and many high school students.

I know it's not proper for a pastor to pat himself on the back when everything seems to have gone so well, but I couldn't help it. In spite of all the tension and rejection I had been feeling, in my estimation this service could not have been better. The testimonies had been right on target, my sermon had covered all the points I thought needed to be covered, and the congregation seemed responsive. What more could I ask?

One wise saying from the book of Proverbs, chapter 16, verse 18, cautions, "Pride goes before destruction, and a haughty spirit before a fall." While I took comfort in how well I had done, I became blind to other reactions that might be festering as people filed out of the pews.

Chapter 23

The flowers at the memorial service had made a beautiful setting, but the decorations in the fellowship hall were even more glorious. The women had outdone themselves in giving the reception the appearance of a festive occasion.

The immediate change of atmosphere from funeral services to the receptions that follow never ceases to amaze me. Even when I have seemed to succeed in focusing the service on the resurrection of the person who has died, a solemnity still reigns, as though that were necessary to properly grieve the loss of the deceased person. Then when I have entered the fellowship hall, I have found people smiling as they enjoyed the food and talked happily about their memories of the deceased.

Such was the case once again. The reception was just as well attended as the memorial service. Since I still basked in my own glow about how the service had gone, I found myself engaging in light chatter with the crowd as I made my way around the room, totally unaware of a verbal time-bomb ticking on the other side of the crowd. Instead, I heard, "Remember when Flora. . . ," and "I'll never forget the time Flora. . ."There were smiles and even laughter.

I made my way to the food table as well. First, I needed to show appreciation to our women who so seriously prepared their delicacies as a sign of their devotion to the church and to the loved one who had died. But I also wanted to check on the tomato aspic—not that I would eat any of it—but to see if it was being well received. Apparently so, from the quantity that had disappeared from the plate and the number of people crowded around it. *Way to go, Jayne.*

I asked myself, *Why am I so concerned about this congregation and how they feel about me? Maybe it only took an appropriate memorial service for Flora and this beautiful reception to get things back on an even keel. This is my church being the church it usually is and can continue to be. I'm at home here. Blow away, clouds of doubt and confusion. Shine, Lord, through the misgivings and uncertainty with hope and joy!*

I felt as though I were walking on air as I continued around the room, giving and receiving smiles and words of encouragement.

When I made my way toward Clifton Stoner, surrounded by members of the family and close friends, I realized something was wrong. No one in this group engaged in smiling chitchat. Some turmoil was building, and Clifton stood at the center of it. My immediate reaction was to avoid the scene, but I knew I couldn't do that. I had to pay my respects to Clifton and to get his reaction to the service.

As I tried to get closer to him, I was met with frowns and heads down, shaking a loud no to me. The crowd around Clifton seemed, at the same time, to be tightening, closing me out. I couldn't tell whether I was being cautioned to go elsewhere by those who gave me fair warning or shielded from him by those sympathetic to his mood. Neither tactic worked, because as soon as he saw me approaching him, he lashed out angrily.

Stoner pushed his way through the guardian circle and faced me. "I've had as much nonsense from you as I can stand," he hissed. "You had a great opportunity to simply praise the woman who was my whole life, and instead you remind us of why she will never be with us again and ask us to be happy about it! And then you give us this feeble plea for forgiveness. I know that boy has died. Good riddance. But it doesn't stop there. What about this mother of his who shaped his life to be the fiend he ended up being?" The smoldering look in his eyes as they narrowed on me told me he wanted revenge and he resented my call for forgiveness.

Completely caught off guard, instead of trying to defend myself, I just sputtered. Just as well. Stoner wasn't interested in a response. He turned and headed out the door.

I sensed danger. His emotional display coupled with his strong disapproval of my incarnation challenge told me it was just a matter of time until Clifton's resentment would explode on Incarnation Church—and on me in particular.

Chapter 24

After I arrived home, I felt devastated. Clifton Stoner's explosion had not gone unnoticed by most of the people in the fellowship hall, including Jayne. She was, of course, sympathetic and supportive but also as perplexed as I had been. She fixed me a cup of coffee as I plunked down on a chair in the breakfast room.

"What could Clifton be thinking? The service couldn't have been better."

I just shook my head, still in a state of unbelief.

"What's going on?" Brandon asked as he came into the room. The children had been out of school since the shooting and, while glad to have the free time, were somewhat at loose ends about how to handle it. Planned holidays were—well—planned.

This time became awkward and unexpected. Hannah had used her time to become more acquainted with Skeeter, but Brandon appeared at a loss about what to do with himself. His wide-eyed look told me he was still in shock and undoubtedly trying to figure the whole shooting thing out. Jayne told me the night before that Brandon had been on the phone with his friends quite a bit. Although he hadn't seemed willing to talk the matter out with his parents, I honestly hoped he found some solace among friends.

In any event, for once he wasn't plugged into his Xbox, and though his mood toward me didn't show a noticeable change, he did sort of become involved in conversation for a few minutes.

"It's just a continuation of what we talked about concerning the church." I sighed. "The situation just gets more complicated. We had a beautiful service for Mrs. Stoner this morning, but Mr. Stoner is furious with me because it wasn't what he wanted it to be. . .even though I tried my best to do it right. I think the thing that rankled him most was that I asked for folks to be forgiving. It's what we Christians are supposed to do regardless of how awful things may be. Mr. Stoner isn't feeling very forgiving right now, and I think I may be near the top of his black list."

Brandon shrugged. "Tyler Wooten's dead. Who else is there for him to be hating so bad?" I saw it as a throwaway line—more of a statement than a question, as though he really didn't care about an answer.

"Tyler's mom. He and, I guess, a lot of other people think she's responsible for what the boy did."

For some reason, that answer seemed to get Brandon's attention, probably because he was still trying to figure out the whole thing himself. He sat down across from me.

"What do you think?"

Wow, he asked my opinion. I folded my hands over my chest, gave him my most serious look, and leaned back into the chair. "I think they're wrong. I've met the woman, and she seems okay to me. She says the problem with Tyler was that he and his dad were really close, and then his dad died. Tyler seemed lost after that and resentful of everything. . .as though he blamed his father for dying. I think Mrs. Wooten did all she could to reach Tyler, but she just couldn't do it. She had no idea he would end up doing what he did."

"Weird." Brandon screwed his mouth to one side.

"Now, to complicate the matter further, I have agreed to have a funeral service for Tyler tomorrow. When Mr. Stoner finds that out, my name really will be mud."

He became more animated, as if to defend me. "Well, what's the big deal about what Mr. Stoner thinks?"

"He is *the* big deal at Incarnation Church. What he says goes. It could mean that I—we—may be the ones who are going."

Shock registered on Brandon's face. "You mean moving, leaving Belvedere, our home, and all our friends?"

Maybe it was a big mistake to bring up such a possibility at that time. My excuse for doing so was probably that Brandon was engaging in a meaningful conversation for the first time in a long time. Maybe that caught me off guard and got my mouth going when I should have been using my brain instead. Anyway, the cat was out of the bag.

Jayne gave me a questioning and troubled look but said nothing.

"We've got to face up to the fact that that could happen as a result of all of this." I reached out to lay my hand on his shoulder. "I'm sorry. Believe me, son, I'm doing the best I can. It's just that things don't always work out as we want them to even when we're trying to do what we believe God wants us to do."

Brandon brushed my hand away with a rotation of his arm, obviously distraught. He had enough to deal with, and now I had added to it.

I returned my arm to the table but continued to have eye contact. "Son, I'd really appreciate it if you wouldn't say anything to Hannah about this. Maybe I shouldn't have said what I did. I may be jumping to conclusions. Things could work out all right."

Jayne broke the somber spell. "If we have to leave, at least Hannah will be able to keep Skeeter."

That obviously gave Brandon no comfort. Shaking his

head, he shuffled out of the room, head bent low.

Jayne wrapped her arms around my neck. "Maybe this is a good time to go see your buddy Philip Treadway. He is someone who can be objective about all of this. I know you've prayed about it and believe you are doing the right thing, but Philip's perspective might be helpful."

So on that Thursday afternoon, I found myself at Treadway's lumberyard.

"Here for another therapy session?" Philip eyed me with an arched brow as he poured me a cup of coffee.

The downcast look on my face undoubtedly clued him in that things were not good.

"Good name for it," I responded. "The last time we talked, I thought of resigning. Now I don't think the choice will be mine. My neck's on the block, and the guillotine could be coming down at any minute."

"What's happened?"

"Clifton Stoner, once again, is what has happened. But if I'm honest, it's more than that."

Philip poured himself a cup of coffee and leaned against the counter. "Tell me more."

"Well, Clifton was quiet about our differences while his

concentration was on Flora's death and burial. Now he's mad as hell, and I seem to be the primary focus."

He raised his finger. "Something must have happened to cause that."

"Yeah." I raised my palms in a sign of frustration. "To him, I made the mistake of calling for forgiveness toward this kid who killed Flora and the others. That's what Christians are supposed to do. And the kid isn't even around anymore. In my sermon at the memorial service, I wanted people to retain happy memories of a really heroic woman who probably saved the lives of others. My sermon honored her in every way I know how. But Clifton only heard the part about forgiving, something he can't do right now."

"Well, where does that leave him? What happened wasn't your fault, and the kid's dead."

I shook my head. "That's not enough for Stoner. He's projecting his furor toward the mother."

Philip set down his cup. "Is there any justification for that?"

"I don't think so. I think the woman did the best she could. The boy loved his dad, they were best pals, did everything together, and his death seemed to leave the boy distraught, hating everyone. Unfortunately, the father had taught Tyler about guns and left him with some."

"How do you know all this?"

I took a sip of coffee, wiped my mouth. "I've met with her. Mrs. Cook, the principal at the high school, asked me to go see her in the hospital, and I did. But I haven't dropped the biggest bombshell on you yet."

He crossed his arms. "What's that?"

"Mrs. Wooten asked me to have a burial service for Tyler, and I agreed to do so."

"Man, you really are a glutton for punishment. You know that this little place of mine is like a crossroads for a lot of guys in this community. They come in here for coffee and conversation, just as you do. I called you and told you about what I have picked up. And I'm telling you, the mood is a violent one. They want to wipe this tragedy out of the minds of the people of Belvedere. That means they want that Wooten woman gone from here, and they want it immediately."

There was a pause, and then Philip's eyes widened as he remembered something. "Did you go to the meeting at the library?"

"Yeah, and the picture you have is all too accurate. So what do you think I should do?"

Philip raised his mug. "Just what you're planning to do."

I raised my eyebrows. *Did he really say that?*

He chuckled. "You know how I feel, or don't feel, about

this Christ of yours. But you either believe what you preach or you don't."

I took a deep breath. "You're right. I didn't come to see you to ask you to change my mind. I wanted confirmation that the situation is as serious as it appears to be. But I also wanted your wisdom in how best to navigate these waters."

"Does Clifton Stoner know about the service for the boy?"

"No, I've had no chance to deal with him on that, and you know how I hate one-on-one confrontation." I grimaced and shook my head.

Philip looked me square in the eyes. "Well, like it or not, that's your first step."

Philip Treadway. My friend. The one guy who was totally honest with me, and I was—as much as I hated it—going to do just what he recommended I do.

I loved this guy as a brother, but I wanted more than anything else for him to be my *Christian* brother. He was raised in the church, but as the story goes, any faith he had disappeared when his young son was killed by a drunk driver.

He had never shared the tragedy with me, and I had never felt led to pry into it. But it reminded me of a similar story a friend had told me long ago. This friend played golf with a guy who knew my friend was a Christian. Even so, he seemed to get pleasure out of cursing God every time something went wrong during the game. My friend knew that this guy had also lost a son in a tragic accident and blamed it on God. Finally, he could stand it no longer.

"God ought to zap you dead right here on the golf course for cursing Him the way you are!" my friend told him. "God didn't kill your son. God gave you your son. He loves you, and He loved your son. But human beings have free will and do bad things. Somebody did a bad thing, and your son's death was a result of it. If we didn't have free will, we would all be like robots. Instead, we are made in the image of God, have minds, and can make choices. Some people make bad choices and bad things happen. We can't control other people's choices, but we can learn to make the right choices ourselves, choices that are in accord with God's will. We learn how to do that by giving our lives to Christ, studying the Bible, praying, worshiping God, and serving others."

My friend told me the man was stunned by this response, but he was also convicted by it and ultimately gave his life to Christ. Deep within him, he had undoubtedly wanted someone to call his bluff and confront him with truth.

Will I ever have that chance with Philip? Well, certainly not in the way my friend had done it with his fellow golfer, because Philip never cursed God. He just, from time to time, made the old Gandhi remark about taking Christianity seriously if he ever found a real Christian. Wasn't that the same thing I aimed for with my incarnation challenge? For us to act like the Christians we are supposed to be?

I mulled over all of this as I headed for a showdown meeting with Clifton Stoner.

Chapter 25

For once in my life, by the grace of God I had the willpower to step up to what I needed to do, and I wasted no time in doing it. I knew it would be a traumatic confrontation with Clifton Stoner. Events were spiraling out of control, so I knew I had to do it immediately. However, I can't deny my surprise when Clifton consented to see me that Thursday evening.

His housemaid, Helen, whom I had seen many times before, cordially received me at the door. She pointed me toward the living room, where Stoner sat in his favorite chair, the lion on his throne.

He made no attempt to stand and greet me as I came into the room and dropped into an overstuffed chair across from him. Instead, he laid the gauntlet of his fury on the line. "I hope you've come to apologize for what you said at the service this morning and to set Incarnation Church back on sound footing rather than trying to take us on some unrealistic 'holier than thou' course."

I sat up straight. "On the contrary, you'll probably want to kick me out of the house by the time we're through."

"What do you mean by that?" Stoner glared at me.

"You're just not going to like what I have to say." I leaned forward to be in direct eye contact with him. "But before I get into any of that, I want you to know that I love you and respect you, even though we often disagree. You've been through an awful shock, something no one should have to suffer. You've not only lost one of the most Christlike individuals I have ever known, a loving wife and mother, and a mainstay of this community. . .but you have lost her in a horrendous way. You need time to heal, if that is ever possible from such a loss."

His jaw twitched. I paused, took a deep breath, and continued. "I wish you wouldn't reach conclusions while you're still dealing with your pain."

He jumped to his feet and paced. "I had already reached my conclusions about the insane way you seem to want to take the church. And if you try to tell me how Flora was a wonderful example of your claim that we Christians should be Christ to the world around us, all I've got to say is, if you're right, that's what killed her. You just as well as said that in your sermon."

Visibly shaken, I slunk back into the chair. His statement caught me by complete surprise. It hadn't occurred to me that Stoner would have thought that through and seen it not as a validation of Flora's life but as my guilt in her death. Dumbfounded by the accusation and unable to make a response, I sat silently looking at the floor to avoid his reproachful look. The longer I did so, the more I felt that Clifton Stoner was convinced he had spoken the truth.

"You have no answer for that," Stoner scoffed and sat back down triumphantly.

I prayed, *Lord, give me the words; You promised to do that in situations like this.* Immediately I perceived the guidance I needed.

I raised my gaze to look straight into his eyes. "Yes, I do have an answer. Whether you'll accept it or not is another matter."

"Try me."

"You undoubtedly knew your wife better than anyone alive. But I question whether you truly understood her spirituality. It is naive to think that what Flora did in giving her life to protect those children was because of any influence I had on her. It was solely because of her relationship with Jesus Christ and the presence and power of the Holy Spirit within her. There is no other answer."

He waved away my comment as though swatting away a fly. "Baloney! You're just trying to get yourself off the hook."

I squared my shoulders and held my ground. "I'm not, but I told you that you might not accept it. As a matter of fact, I think you would have done the same thing Flora did, faced with the same situation."

With intensity in his glare, Stoner ignored the last part of my remark. "Well, I know you went through the motions of having a nice memorial service for Flora, despite most of your sermon, but I have to be bluntly honest, as you know I always am. I don't want you as my pastor anymore. It's time for a change at Incarnation."

Without letting that bomb blow me away, I gave him a glare equal to his own. "I'm sorry you feel that way. But since you're being so honest, I must be honest with you. I'm going to have a funeral service for that boy, Tyler Wooten."

Clifton Stoner exploded, shaking with rage. "You are out of your mind!" he shouted. "Surely you know you can't have anything like that at Incarnation for that child of the devil and his god-awful mother."

"The service wouldn't be at Incarnation, but our people will find out about it, and I know how much it will hurt my favor with some members of our church. But I don't believe I have much choice. I was asked to do it, I am a clergyman, and I believe an ordained Christian is the one to perform the service. It may not do Tyler Wooten any good, but it may be a way to reach his mother. It's worth a try, and it is the right thing to do."

Clifton Stoner pointed a shaking finger at me as though it were a weapon. "Get out of here! I wish I never had to see you again."

Chapter 26

Back home, I sat in our family room surrounded by my little family facing its first major crisis.

I looked around the room as though seeing it for the first time. This had been home to us for fifteen years, and now it appeared we would be leaving. It wasn't much of a home by commercial standards, but Jayne had chosen well in filling it with what we needed and what we loved. As I looked around, I noticed mementos, things we had bought on special trips to remind us of those good times. Also the pictures of us as a family, especially the children at various stages of their growth. I even noticed the worn places on the furniture and rugs put there through our enjoyment and use. And the walls I had painted more than once and cabinets I had repaired over the years. It was a comfortable room in a comfortable house, and we would hate to leave it.

Jayne and I had always believed it was best to involve the children in serious issues we faced. Once they had been old enough to sense when we were under tension, it seemed best to get everything out on the table. This time Jayne took the lead.

"We've got to stick together, troops. Belvedere is not a big place, and people are going to be talking, saying things we won't like hearing. But that's not the worst part. We just need to get ready for it."

Hannah cocked her head in a way she did when puzzled with a math problem. "Ready for what, Mama?"

Jayne glanced briefly at me to see if I wanted to answer. "Your dad may be asked to step down as pastor of the church. And that would mean that we would be losing this house and moving somewhere else."

"Where would we go?" Her lips began to quiver.

I stepped into the discussion at that point. "We don't know, honey. We'll just have to see."

With a bleak look on his face, Brandon remained silent. He already knew what was going on, but Hannah was clearly bewildered by the whole thing.

"What's happened? What's caused this?"

Jayne reached for her hand. "Misunderstandings mostly. Your father has an important position in this community, and he has had to do and say some things that people will disagree with. We'll just have to see how it all works out, but we wanted you to know what is going on. Particularly if you hear people saying unkind things about your father.

He is going to hold a funeral service for that boy Tyler, and a lot of people will resent that."

Hannah swiveled to me, her forehead wrinkled. "Why do you have to do that?"

"Someone has to do it, and I was the one who was asked."

"But Dad, can't you get someone else to do it?"

"I don't believe I can, honey. How do you feel when someone says they'll do something you want them to do and then they let you down? And how do you think I'd feel going around begging some other pastor to do what I was unwilling to do?"

In the meantime, Brandon, though still not saying a thing, became more restless. His expression darkened as he continued inwardly to deal with matters that seemed so unreal to him. Within the week he had been confronted with violent, unimaginable sudden death among his classmates. His school life had been disrupted as a result, and now he faced being shamed out of town because of what I had done.

Finally, his thoughts burst through. "This whole thing sucks! It's not fair. Why is this happening to me?"

"It's happening to *all of us*, Brandon. You're right that it's not fair, but we have to stick together and make the best of it we can."

I was glad Jayne had responded before I could. I swallowed my anger. I heard my seminary pastoral counselor's wisdom in my head. *Teenagers are often self-oriented. It's all part of the growing-up process.*

Brandon mumbled something that sounded like profanity and stormed out of the room. Deep down, I wondered if, in addition to everything else, he blamed me for getting us into a situation I could have easily avoided.

Hannah looked tearfully and wide-eyed at Jayne and me. Her world was also falling apart.

I pulled her into a hug. "Somehow, sweetheart, it will all work out. Maybe not like we want it to, but we know God has plans for us. Let's try to look forward to what they might be."

Chapter 27

O n the Monday afternoon of the shooting, I had gone into the intensive care room at the hospital and prayed for Tyler after the doctor had informed Connie that the attempt to save him had failed. Having agreed to do a service for Tyler, I told her that the one for Flora Stoner would have to come first. Connie understood and said that her brother, who lived in a neighboring town, would make arrangements for the body in the meantime at the local funeral parlor. She would wait for my call concerning further arrangements. In the days that followed, after an exchange of telephone calls, Friday morning at ten was decided on as the time for the service.

I met with Connie Wooten at nine thirty at the funeral parlor chapel where the service would be held. The first step in the process was looking the place over and getting the lay of the land. And even that didn't lie well.

Part of it was my fault. A funeral parlor as a substitute

for a church seemed so phony at times like this. Where the overwhelming smell of flowers didn't permeate the rooms, the smell of furniture wax did. Everything was always too neat, and the smiles of the staff seemed glued on.

Over the years I had had many dealings with funeral homes, including this one. Usually the funeral service would be held in the church, but the bereaved often wanted their pastor with them when making the arrangements at the funeral home. And almost always, the people at the funeral home were overly gracious. They recognized what those who had lost a loved one were going through, and they wanted to impress on them their sympathy and their care for detail.

Such was not the case in this instance. The people at the funeral home were standoffish, to say the least. They were doing something they were expected to do, but they weren't happy about doing it. The frozen smiles were the best we got. Connie Wooten showed real character in being able to size up what was going on and not comment on it.

Accepting the situation and preparing for the service itself, I needed to say some things to Connie in advance.

"Connie, before this service starts, there are things we need to talk about. Even though this is taking place in a funeral home, it is going to be a Christian service. Are you a Christian?"

She looked away. "I'd say that I was, but I don't know I really am. My parents didn't go to church or show any signs of being Christians, but they'd probably have said they were Christians, too. The only time I ever went in a church was with school friends who would talk me into going to Sunday school and youth activities with them from time to time. Lou and I got married in a church by promising the pastor that we would attend, but then it just seemed like too much trouble. Though I had to work some Sundays, that was the only day both of us ever had off from work, so it was time we spent with each other and with Tyler."

"Let me put it another way. Do you remember being baptized, and have you ever given your life to Jesus Christ as your Lord and Savior?"

Connie seemed thoughtful for a moment as she reflected back on her life. "No, I don't remember anything like that. But I knew enough about Jesus to know that He wanted us to do the right thing, and that's what I've tried to do."

Same old story. I remembered how, in my own life, I had thought that Christianity was simply about living a moral life. So I had tried to "do the right thing" just like Connie in order to be acceptable to God. It was only after Christ had burst into my life that I realized my focus had been one of pure selfishness, trying to manipulate God by appearing always to do the right thing. And then the Holy Spirit had convicted me of my selfishness—how I had always taken the moral high ground because that was what worked for me. It made me look good in the eyes of others, but in truth I had seldom shown love and compassion for others.

"That's how I used to look at things, too, Connie. Jesus does want us to live a moral life, but faith is so much more than that. God isn't a judge who lives up in the sky checking to see if we do more good things than bad. God loves us and wants to be in contact with us. Just like in that old story about Adam and Eve, God knows that we are selfish by nature. But because He wants to be in relationship with us, He sent His Son, Jesus Christ, to live and die for us, that our selfishness might be forgiven and we might be right with him. When we give ourselves to Jesus, it's a whole new way of life, and it is an eternal life. We will be with God forever."

I didn't expect this simple Gospel presentation to lead Connie Wooten to a sudden conversion, but I hoped it would get her thinking along the right path.

She nodded, her eyes soft. "Thanks, I never looked at it that way." Then her face paled. "But what about Tyler? As far as I know, he didn't really know anything about Jesus."

I gave her an empathetic smile. "God knows what it's

like to lose a son. Let's entrust Tyler to Him."

The contrast between the service for Flora Stoner and the one for Tyler Wooten was stark. There were no flowers, and to say the service was sparsely attended would be an exaggeration. In attendance, other than Connie and myself, were Connie's brother and sister-in-law, two friends of Connie's from work, two neighbors from her trailer park, the high school principal, Mrs. Cook, and Jayne, who had come to be supportive of me.

But there was a major—and unwelcome—surprise. Seated at the very back of the funeral parlor chapel were Clifton Stoner and two other members of the Incarnation Church board. They sat, stony-faced and arms crossed, there to observe who might be in attendance and to hear what I would say. Silent purveyors of disapproval and judgment.

As disconcerting as this hostile presence felt, I couldn't let it affect what I planned to say. When the recorded music ended, I got to my feet, looked out on the tiny group sitting together in the front of the chapel, and began. "Dear ones, let's be honest with one another—we are here in shock, speechless and heartbroken."

Connie Wooten, whose life had fallen apart and who had already shed so many tears, let her grief flow in another shower of sorrow as her brother put an arm around her in an attempt to comfort her.

I read Psalm 46, through the eighth verse, then explained the meaning. "Despite what has happened, God is in charge. He truly is 'our refuge and our strength, a very present help in trouble,' and this is a time of trouble for us because we can't understand how all of this could have happened. But God is merciful and just and will do what is right because it is His nature to do so. As I told Connie before this service, God knows what it is like to lose a son because He gave His Son, Jesus, to show us how much He loves us. Let's lean into that love."

Connie looked up at me through the tears, and everyone else focused on my words, including the three in the back—though they smirked in disbelief at my message.

Encouraged by Connie's group, I then read Isaiah 61:1–3. "This passage from the Old Testament tells us of the nature of God. Jesus quoted from this passage when He taught in His hometown, saying that it was being fulfilled in their very presence. In other words, Jesus completed in His life what God had promised all along—to preach good news to the poor, freedom for those in prison, sight for the blind and release of the oppressed. That's us, folks. We're the ones who are poor, in prison, blind, and oppressed until we come into a right relationship with God through Jesus Christ. But God is here for us regardless."

There was some restlessness among the attendants at

this point. I didn't know their faith background. They may not have liked the categories I was placing them in, but I continued. "It's God's nature to comfort those who mourn. We need an extra measure of that comfort because of the circumstances. I pray that you will sense that comfort in your lives and that you will bring some good from this tragedy by giving your lives to Jesus Christ so that the service at your death may be one of celebration because you have entered eternity with God. And I'm available to any of you who are ready to make that commitment."

The three in the back of the room continued to glare. The others glanced back and forth at one another, but no one moved.

I paused and smiled. "Now, let's adjourn to the grave site where we can put Tyler's body to rest."

At the brief graveside service—which the three Incarnation people did not attend—I prayed, "O God, whose mercies cannot be numbered, accept our prayers on behalf of Tyler Wooten, whose tortured mind led him astray. We place him in Your loving hands. May he rest in a peace that he could not find on this earth. And bless his mother, Connie, who loved him, that she may find peace in this world and in the world to come. Amen."

Following the service, three things happened. Connie's brother tried to give me an honorarium in compensation for performing the service. I appreciated the thought but felt it would have been inappropriate to accept anything— even on behalf of Incarnation Church. So I thanked him for his thoughtfulness but declined. Much more significantly, Connie asked me to pray for her to receive Jesus Christ as her Lord and Savior. Then she asked me to come by her home later in the day to talk about some things she wasn't comfortable discussing with her family and others around.

As she had requested, I met with Connie Wooten in her somewhat dilapidated home in the local trailer park in the early afternoon. The area was decidedly run-down. The other trailers scattered around the park showed the same degree of wear as Connie's: paint peeling off, rust showing through in some places and mold in others, scraggly grass and weeds, clutter everywhere. Connie's aged little car was parked next to the side of the house.

I couldn't help but compare Connie's living conditions with those of Otis Huntington on the other side of town. Both were in bad repair, showing age, reflecting the low economic status of those who lived there and perhaps their hopelessness. Of course this was a trailer park and Otis had lived in an apartment complex. That was one difference, but there was another. Otis's neighborhood was the scene of drugs and danger, whereas this area seemed calm and peaceful. At least for now.

Connie met me at the door, slump-shouldered and fidgety, as she led me into her small "everything room"—entry way, living/family room, breakfast/dining room, and kitchen all rolled into one. The furniture was well worn but not soiled, and the few possessions she had were neatly placed around the room. It had the sweet smell of soap. The area around Connie's trailer might be shabby, but she was personally clean and tidy.

Connie offered coffee. Once we were settled around the Formica-topped breakfast table in metal folding chairs with mugs of coffee in front of us, she straightened in her chair but looked at me with puppy dog eyes. "Mr. Long, what am I going to do?"

"First of all, I think it's time for you to start calling me Steve. I'm going to be your friend through all of this. I want you to bring me up-to-date on what's been happening that we didn't have a chance to talk about this morning." I gave her a reassuring smile. "But I also want to remind you that you indicated you want to accept Jesus Christ as your Savior, and I want to help you do that."

"St–St–Steve"—she paused, unsure of our new relationship—"I've lost my job and have no means of income—"

Before she could say more, I interrupted. "I may have lost mine as well."

The shock on her face spoke for itself, but she asked anyway. "Surely not because of me. . .you doing the service for Tyler?"

I patted her hand. "No, other things going on at church." Well, in a sense, it was only a half-truth, but the woman was carrying enough burden. "Losing your job is a tough deal. What a lousy thing to happen in the middle of all you have lost. I imagine you are wondering why anyone would want you to suffer more than you already have. It's sure easy to get disappointed with the human race at times like this."

Connie sat there with fear in her eyes and hesitation in her manner, and I realized there was more she wanted to say.

"I'm getting threats about getting out of town."

I knew it was coming, but I felt it best to play ignorant until I heard it from her own mouth. "What kind of threats?"

"Nasty ones. Phone calls and even a brick thrown at the trailer with a note on it: 'Get out of town or you'll be sorry.'"

I took a deep breath, trying to tamp down my anger and frustration at the meanness of the small-minded people who had threatened to harm her and were carrying out that threat. Here was this helpless, distraught woman being bullied by Mike Troutman and possibly others out of vengeance for something she had not done, something that had destroyed her life. The injustice of it all was beyond me.

"Connie, this is so unfair. I can't explain how people can be like this. Ignorance may be an excuse, I don't know. I guess we need a strategy to deal with it, some way to get you some protection."

Connie just shook her head, the picture of despair.

"Let me have that note and the brick so I can take them to Clyde Matthews, the police chief."

She sighed. "I will, but he probably wants me gone from here as much as anyone else. You know he and another policeman came by and questioned me the day after the shooting. They said they just wanted to try to figure out the circumstances of why and how Tyler did it so as to prevent something like that in the future. But I felt like they were treating me as a criminal.

"They tore Tyler's room apart and questioned me for what seemed like hours. Then they took any weapons that were still in the trailer." She screwed up her face and looked on the verge of rage. "I didn't want them, but what authority did they have for doing that, and what are they going to do with them?"

Once she had gotten onto the topic of the police, Connie became more animated and agitated, her voice quivering with emotion as she related the events. This woman, in spite of everything, was tired of being a doormat. She had some backbone! And some heat with regard to the police chief.

"In addition to all that, everyone seems to be shunning me. Former friends, neighbors—they don't talk to me, don't look at me, act as though I don't exist. What *am* I going to do?"

"What about your brother and sister-in-law? Can't you go live with them?"

"Not really. Their little house is already overcrowded with them and their children. They have no place for me, and Bill doesn't have much income. He was a great help in paying for Tyler's funeral, but there isn't anything else."

"If things weren't so bad on my end, I might be able to offer you a job. We're always in need of good workers around the church, but that's out of the picture right now."

I knew I didn't have an answer for her, but I needed to do what I could, at least for the moment. I opened my wallet and gave Connie some money.

Her eyes widened, her forehead wrinkled. "I can't take this."

"You don't have much choice. Until we can figure something out, you've got to survive."

Her body shook slightly and her face contorted, tears forming in her eyes. "I can't stay here. What can I do?"

"Again, you don't seem to have much choice. It wouldn't work for you to come live with us because we're in turmoil right now ourselves, even though, if things continue to get worse, of course you could stay with us for a few days. Let me go see Chief Matthews to find out if we can get you some protection."

Based on her episode with the police chief, she was about to give me a "lots of luck" response. I redirected our conversation. "Let's talk about where you are about committing your life to the Lord."

Frankly, I didn't know what to do about this woman and the problems she faced. It might seem to some a cop-out to shift from the practical to the spiritual, but as a pastor, it was my natural focus and the most important thing I could do at that moment.

Connie's face bloomed into wonderment. "You know I don't really know anything about being a real Christian. It's just that you showed me something about what God is really like by what you've said and done in my situation. And my life is a complete mess. I know that something is missing, and I want it. It looks to me like God is the answer."

I sat forward in my chair. "Okay, let me put it this way. This is what I say to people who seem to be where you are.

Admit a need for God in your life. Then ask Him to come into your heart and make you whole. You can do that with a simple prayer such as: 'Lord, please accept me as I am and make me into the person You want me to be.' Would you be willing to pray this?"

Connie hesitated then said, "I think I can, but there's a lot more that I will need to learn to know what all of that means. And what will happen to me when I pray that prayer?"

She became animated, pressing me. "Will I feel anything? Will I hear God speaking to me?"

I took a breath. "The essential thing, Connie, is having your heart in the right place. God is calling you to come to Him through a commitment like this; it's His idea. If that speaks to your heart, you are ready to make the commitment even though there is so much you don't understand. I've been a Christian for many years and have even gone to a school to teach me more so that I could be a pastor, but there's still a great deal more that I don't know. We are to spend our lives studying the Bible, praying, worshiping with other Christians, and serving others in Christ's name in order to grow in our relationship with God. But we all have to start somewhere."

Looking her directly in the eyes, I continued, "I can't tell you exactly what will happen when you pray that prayer.

God works with each of us in different ways. You may feel a warmness come over you, or you may not. Anything can happen, but whatever it is will be good. The main thing that will happen is that you should feel some sense of peace even in the midst of all the bad things going on in your life. That's because you will be a new person, a new person in Christ."

Connie expelled her breath loudly. "Well, I really don't understand it all, but I'm ready to pray if you will sort of lead me."

I gave her a reassuring look. "Just repeat after me: 'Lord, please accept me as I am, and make me into the person You want me to be.'"

Connie bowed her head, closed her eyes, and said the prayer and then somewhat amazingly and tearfully added: "And Lord, look after Tyler. He did a terrible thing. I don't know how he could have done such a terrible thing, but he did, and many people are suffering because of it. Forgive me for not having been a better mother to him. Forgive me now for worrying about myself. Let me put all of this in Your hands. Thank You."

"That was just right, Connie. Now let's see what the Lord is going to do with all of this."

As I drove away from Connie's, the sun broke through. It blended with the hope—almost joy—I was feeling in my heart. In the midst of all the things that seemed to be going wrong, Connie's prayer was like that blaze of sunshine. God had brought this woman from heartbreaking tragedy to new life in Him. Something was going right, and God gave me the privilege of being a part of it. My mood shifted from high anxiety to anticipating the challenges ahead.

Chapter 28

My next stop was the Belvedere Police Station, located in what is called the Municipal Center—a rather high and fancy name for anything in Belvedere. The center consisted of the municipal court, the city clerk's office, and other city offices. The building was one of the newer ones in town, six or so years old, although it was really a renovation of the old Moose Lodge. The police office was downstairs in an area that had once, ironically, been a bar.

I had been impressed with the way the police handled the shooting at the high school. They were quickly on the scene and professional in sorting things out in the midst of chaos, especially when surrounded by other law enforcement, fire, and emergency responders from all over the area.

I didn't know Clyde Matthews, the police chief. He had only held the office for a little over a year. During that time I had had no direct contact with him, including on the day of the shooting.

The police sergeant on duty received me cordially and buzzed the chief's office to see if he was available to see me. He told me how to get to the chief's office. I guess I expected the chief to come out and meet me in the hallway, but he didn't. Instead, as I entered his office I saw a large man casually seated behind a well-ordered desk with a smirk on his face.

"Chief Matthews, I am Steve Long of Incarnation Church."

The policeman had a sour look on his face, shifted his position in his chair, and said in a flippant manner, "Yeah, I know who you are." Matthews didn't get up to shake my hand, making it clear I was an unwelcome visitor.

"That doesn't get us off to a very good start when I wanted to congratulate you on the way your guys handled the situation at the high school on the day of the shooting." Actually I wanted to say a lot more, considering the way he had apparently treated Connie Wooten, but now was not the time to get into an argument with him or to otherwise antagonize him.

"Sorry," he said in a way that didn't sound like he was. He clicked off his computer and leaned back in his chair. "What can I do for you?"

He hadn't offered me a seat, so I remained standing in front of his desk. "I've just come from Connie Wooten's.

She's being threatened. Most of it has come from phone calls, but this brick and note hit her trailer last night." I tried to hand the items to him. His unwillingness to reach forward to accept them gave me a "so what?" message, so I set them down on his desk.

Trying to look undeterred by his disinterest, I continued, "Two things. I'm wondering if you can figure out who threw this, and I'm hoping you can give her some protection."

"You're trying to put me between a rock and a hard place, preacher." The chief huffed through his cheeks. "The fact is, the people of Belvedere probably don't want the woman hurt, but they sure as heck want her gone. You'd be a lot more help to her and to the rest of us if you'd just talk her into leaving."

I could feel my frustration and anger building once again. How could it be that with every corner I turned I seemed to meet with opposition, disappointment, defeat? The top man in my church had apparently become my enemy, and now the top man in law enforcement refused to take his job seriously and toyed with me in the process.

I could feel the heat in my face. "But Mrs. Wooten has no place to go, and it's your job as chief of police of this town to protect her."

There was a long silence as Chief Matthews seemed to

be weighing his options. "You don't really think having this brick and note is going to tell me anything, do you? We're not a big city police force with a forensic lab and all that stuff, and I don't think we could make anything of this if we did. And how many policemen do you think I have? I don't have teams of guys who can guard people around the clock like they do on those cop shows on TV."

"I'm not talking about round-the-clock protection." I forced a smile. "What I'm concerned about is what might happen after dark. Surely you could have a patrol car come through the trailer park during the night."

"Even in our little town, we've got some serious drug stuff going on at night, and it's not in the trailer park. We have to put the men we have where the greatest danger is."

I seemed to be fighting a losing battle, but I refused to walk away from it as easily as he wanted. So I simply stood there, my eyes glued on his face.

He pushed his chair back, raised his head toward the ceiling, and rolled his eyes as he let out a big breath. "Okay, okay, I'll see what I can do; but I still say that the best thing you can do is get her out of here."

"Thanks." *For nothing.*

Chapter 29

After leaving Clyde Matthews's office, I had a brainstorm. Why not go see Charles Barnett, the editor of the local paper, the *Belvedere Herald*? Barnett, though only a Christmas and Easter Christian, was a member of Incarnation.

I was fortunate to find him in. Maybe things would start going in the right direction after all.

For a small-town publication, the *Herald* did well. A twice-a-week paper, it was printed in Atlanta and shipped to Belvedere for delivery. The quality of the articles, ads, and other features was excellent, and it apparently had wide subscribership throughout the area. Belvedere was proud of its hometown newspaper.

It wasn't the first time I had been in Charles Barnett's office, but I remained impressed. It was a welcoming presence. As might be expected, the large mahogany desk, with the comfortable chair and credenza behind it, dominated the room. But the front part of the room contained plush leatherette armchairs arranged around a coffee table. This provided a place where Barnett could meet with visitors or staff in an informal setting. Bookcases filled with a great variety of books lined the walls. For a small-town newspaper editor, Charles Barnett was an educated man.

As I came into the room, Barnett rose from his desk and met me with a smile and a firm handshake. A handsome man in his late fifties, he showed the early stages of a weight problem but generally seemed healthy and in good spirits.

He pointed me to one of the armchairs and sat across from the coffee table, offering to get us some coffee, which I declined. With the formalities behind us, Barnett's face became more somber as though he sensed I was not making a social call. "What's going on?"

"A lot!" I shifted my body from side to side in the chair, trying to get comfortable.

Barnett, who undoubtedly had an ear for whatever was going on in Belvedere, decided to try again. "Is there a problem at church? I hope not. You're the best pastor we've ever had. I know you can't prove it by me because I miss church so often. But you know how it is. My work just interferes with regular attendance on Sunday mornings."

I could have argued with him on that, because he knew it was rationalization and not truth that he spoke. But for now I had something much more urgent on my mind.

"Well, thanks for the kind words, but that's not why I'm here. I'm here because of something tied into the shooting at the high school. Connie Wooten, the mother of the shooter, isn't a bad person. Even so, the people of Belvedere—or at least some of them—want her out of town and seem to be threatening violence if she stays. I've talked with Chief Matthews about it but received a lukewarm response, to say the least."

"What can I do?"

"What can you do? As editor of the paper, you can influence thought in this community. Can't you write an editorial that calls for understanding and reconciliation? Or at least calm the waters?"

He tented his fingers in a thoughtful pose. Good sign. At least he seemed more receptive than the police chief had been.

"Maybe." He shrugged. "In truth, what I might say in the paper probably has a lot less influence than people think. I wish it weren't so, but I have to be realistic about it. What I write is just my opinion, and others are free to have their own. But let me think about it."

I thanked him.

"Now," he continued, "give me your reading on what people are thinking."

"Normally fair-minded people like Clifton Stoner feel strongly that Connie Wooten's continued presence in the community is a constant reminder of what her son did, something that will grieve the people of this town for years to come. I understand that, even though I don't agree with it. But there are others who have revenge on their minds. Not only has Mrs. Wooten gotten threatening phone calls, but a brick was thrown against her trailer with a note telling her to get out of town or face the consequences. In the meantime, she's been fired from her job—again, as a vengeful act—so she has no money and no place to go."

Barnett tapped his finger on his chin. I waited. After a few moments, he nodded, I think more to himself than me. "It's a dilemma all right. Let me see what I can do."

I rose to shake his hand. "I'd be grateful," I said. "I understand why people don't want Mrs. Wooten around, but what happened wasn't her fault. I've gotten to know her a little bit. She's basically a good person, but she has lost everything." I counted off with my fingers. "First, her husband to cancer, then her son, now her job. What's more, she has become a Christian from a totally secular background. She wants to do the right thing. Now isn't a time for her to be thrown to the wolves."

Barnett nodded once more and repeated himself. "Okay, let me see what I can do."

Chapter 30

My next stop was Philip Treadway's lumberyard. It was time to bring my friend up-to-date on what was happening—as though Philip wouldn't already know almost all of it.

I sat at the coffee counter while Philip dealt with a handful of customers, who averted their eyes from me. After he'd assisted them, he came over.

"Remember the good old days, Steve? Those times when you would come around and we'd tell jokes and talk about all the good things happening in Belvedere? Different story now, huh?"

"Sadly, that's just the way it is." I leaned my hands on the counter. "Once again I'm here to give you all the bad news, if there is any you don't already know."

"Shoot." Philip cringed, immediately sorry for such a wrong choice of words.

I waved it away with a nervous chuckle. Then my face became serious again. "I had the confrontation with

Clifton. It ended with his saying he wished he never had to see me ever again, or words to that effect. Then he and two other members of the church board showed up at the service for Tyler Wooten, looking like executioners waiting for the hanging."

Before I could continue, Philip broke in. "Situation's going from bad to worse."

"I'll say!"

He shook his head then looked me straight in the eyes. "Tell me the worse."

"Connie Wooten is being threatened, and the police chief doesn't seem to be interested in doing anything about it. I guess that and my situation are the two immediate crises."

"Steve, you've gotten to know a lot about Belvedere in the years you've been here, but you haven't learned all the family connections. Mike Troutman is undoubtedly the main force behind the threats to the Wooten woman, and he is Police Chief Clyde Matthews's favorite nephew. And that means Matthews has lost a loved one—Mike's daughter—in the shooting."

Another punch below the belt. Everything seemed stacked against Connie Wooten. "You're right. I had no idea. I've seen Troutman in action, but tell me more about this guy."

"Troutman's daughter, as I said, was killed in the shooting, so he has reason to want to do something. But he's also a hothead who would find it easy enough to do something really stupid."

"So, from your vantage point—and you always seem to have a good one—what does this mean?"

"It means that these guys will ultimately take some deadly action against the Wooten woman if she doesn't leave town. And the police, because of Clyde Matthews, will do nothing to prevent it."

I gasped. "*Deadly* action?"

"My guess is that they would grab her, probably rough her up a bit, drive her to some remote place, and throw her out. Worse still, they would burn her out of her home."

I was at a loss for words. After absorbing this, I tried a new approach. "Would it do any good for me to go talk with Troutman?"

"None. Total waste of time."

"Is there nothing we can do?"

"Well, let's think about it." Philip tilted his head, closed his eyes, and gave the matter some thought.

I'm always amazed at how he seemed to be able to wrestle through issues and come up with practical solutions, although I wasn't sure I would be happy with the results this time.

After a few minutes of contemplation, Philip looked directly at me and said as though he were still working out the matter in his mind, "Two things. First, I know the sheriff, Don Jones, over in Davisville. I'll call him and let him know about the threats against Mrs. Wooten and Clyde Matthews's reluctance to do anything about them, and see what he thinks we should do.

"Second," he continued, "the guys who are making the threats won't try anything during the daytime. They'll wait for darkness, ply themselves with beer or whiskey to work up their so-called courage, then do whatever they decide to do. So, someone needs to be keeping an eye out for the Wooten woman in the early hours of the night, and—because of Clyde Matthews—it won't be the police."

"Who, then?"

Philip pointed at my chest. "You take tonight, and I'll take tomorrow night."

I hated to admit it, but in addition to being nonconfrontational, I thought of myself as a coward in other ways as well. I've never been one for physical violence. Even my participation in sports had been volleyball, which should tell you something about me.

"What good would that do? I mean, if it's a gang, how would we stop them?"

"Just being there as an eyewitness to what they are

about could put a stop to it. Plus, we've both got cell phones and can call for help."

It all sounded rather doubtful to me, but I couldn't let Philip see my faintheartedness. After all, why was he willing to stick his neck out? I saw the problem as mine. I was the one who befriended Connie Wooten. As far as I knew, Philip had never even seen the woman. Was this just friendship and concern for me, or was he testing me to see if I would live up to my incarnation challenge? I considered some way to bail out, but I was in a corner and knew no option but to agree with his plan.

Trying to sound confident rather than allowing my voice to crack, I found myself saying, "Okay. If you're really willing to do that, I will, too."

Before I left the store, we made some tactical decisions about calls we might make from our cell phones if we needed help. Obviously, Chief Matthews would not be on our list.

Chapter 31

When I finally got home from all the stuff I dealt with all day, Jayne's embrace at the front door held an extra measure of love and understanding for what I was working through. But it was also the hug of someone reaching for safety in what seemed like a desperate situation. In the back of her mind, I know the question was, *What are we going to do?*

Though we both showed signs of mental and physical exhaustion, I knew my wife would want me to hold nothing back. I tried to fill her in on all of the things that happened that very eventful day.

She physically deflated, almost like the air going out of a balloon. "I'm trying not to panic about the situation, but what do you really think is going to happen?"

I looked at the floor. "I have no idea. Philip Treadway thinks I should go plant a church, one in which people are told upfront about the incarnation challenge."

"Is that realistic?" was Jayne's practical question. "Where

would it be, here or somewhere else?"

"I don't know, sweetheart. Truth be told, I'm just grasping at straws at this point. We've got to have faith. And look, you're the strong one in this family. While I'm flailing around trying to figure out what is going on and what to do about it, I'm counting on you to keep me on track."

"Ha!" She poked me in the chest. "If you're counting on me for much more than just loving you and the children and trying to be adaptable to whatever happens, you're leaning on a weak reed."

I tried not to chuckle. She hardly was that in my book. When I think of Jayne's strengths, I'm sometimes reminded of that old joke about the guy who claimed that he made all the important decisions in his family. "Like what?" the other guy asks.

"Well, like how our country should be handling international affairs, who's going to win the World Series, things like that."

"Then what are the minor things your wife decides?"

"Oh, stuff like where we'll live, what kind of house we'll live in, how many children we'll have, where they'll go to school. . .just the small stuff."

I took her in my arms and kissed her on the forehead. "Weak reed? I don't think so, Miss Practical. You're the rudder on this little boat we're sailing. So, wherever we're headed, we'll get there safely."

She shook her head and said, "Well, you know where my strength comes from, and yours, too." She pulled us both to our knees right there in the kitchen. Why hadn't I thought of that? I had been putting all my faith in a guy who had great wisdom but was mad at God!

Following our prayers for the Lord's guidance, we got to our feet in a hug. Jayne looked up at me with a wrinkled brow. "I just have this sense of impending doom. I know that by God's grace we can cope with whatever might happen, but it's the tension of waiting for the other shoe to drop that's wearing me down."

"Things do seem to be getting out of hand, if they weren't already." I took her hand in mine. "We've had a lot to deal with in a very short period of time. Otis committed suicide because he was lonely, and I still feel guilty about that. Then this horrendous thing happens to Belvedere, something that will scar these people for the rest of their lives whether or not they lost family or loved ones in that shooting. You and I have lost Flora Stoner, who was one of the best people we've ever known, and yet her husband has somehow become our archenemy. I've somehow gotten tangled up with the Wootens, doing what I thought was right. Some in the community are looking for blood, Jayne. They've already gotten Connie Wooten fired from her job, as though that was going to solve anything. Clifton Stoner was ready to have me fired over the incarnation challenge, and now he thinks I'm in cahoots with the devil, blaming me for Flora's death and for having the funeral service for the boy. In the midst of all of this, I challenged the people of Incarnation Church to show the world that Christ is still alive, and that completely backfired. Somehow I feel like all of this is converging on us, and who knows what Clifton Stoner will do next."

It didn't take long to find out. The phone rang, and it was Stoner.

"I'm calling, Steve, to tell you that you're fired. We want you out of your house within thirty days and out of the lives of us Incarnation folks as well."

Although I suspected this was going to happen, I felt nonetheless stunned. I stood in silence, the phone in my hand for a few moments, and then just hung up.

Tears welled up in my eyes. I told Jayne, "It's happened. That was Stoner. The board has voted us out. We have thirty days."

Jayne's hands flew to her face. "Oh no! I know you thought this might happen, but it can't be! How could they? Surely they could have handled it in a more gracious way. Couldn't they have just said they think it's time for you to move on to another church and help you find the right one?

Thirty days? That's not even Christian!"

I drew her to me as she sobbed. "People are people, sweetheart. I'm sure it wasn't a unanimous vote, but so what? The end result is the same."

"How can you find another church if you've been fired from this one? What about the children? This is so unfair to them. They've been through enough with the shooting, and now this."

Before I could answer, the doorbell rang. It was the minority report from the board meeting—Ann Boronski, Arnie Dixon, and Paul Rivers were at the door. Ann was the only female on the board and leader of the women's prayer group in the church. Arnie was a farmer and one of the most serious Bible students at Incarnation. Paul was a well-respected doctor in the community and head of the welcoming committee at church. The defeated looks on their faces told the story as Jayne ushered them into our family room and got them seated.

"Oh, Steve." Paul wrung his hands. "We're so sorry. We did everything we could, but it was no use. Clifton has the other three members of the board in his pocket, and he was out for blood."

"Yeah, he just called. Tell us about it."

Ann took the lead. "You're aware that Clifton and a couple of other board members showed up at the service for

Tyler Wooten. An emergency meeting of the Incarnation Church board was called immediately afterward. It was at Stoner's house. . .just him and the other six board members without you."

Ann was standing on one foot and then the other, with Paul and Arnie fidgeting behind her. I could see this was going to take some time. "Sit down and make yourselves comfortable."

They arranged themselves around the family room, and Ann continued. "We guessed something was afoot when you weren't there. Smug would be the best way to describe the look of those who were already seated. They knew why they were there, and the decisions made would please them."

Arnie stepped into the story at that point. "As soon as the three of us were seated and before Stoner could say a word, Paul leaned on the table with a laser focus on Stoner and asked, 'Why is our pastor not here?'

"Clifton shook his head and said our bylaws provide for executive sessions when dealing with issues concerning our pastor. So we wanted to know what issues, because we didn't know of any issues that needed to be discussed behind your back."

Paul wanted to get his two bits worth in. "That's when Stoner said we were there to ask for your resignation as pastor. We couldn't believe it. We told them that you're the best thing that ever happened to Incarnation and we wanted to know what this was all about."

Paul was getting up steam. "In his self-assured manner, Clifton told us there were two reasons you had to go. First, he got off on your sermon this past Sunday. He said you are off track by thinking we human beings who have to struggle just to be halfway decent Christians should all of a sudden be Christ to those around us. As he was telling us all this, he was shaking his head, rolling his eyes, and waving the back of his hand at us, sloughing off your challenge as though it weren't worthy of any consideration. He even pointed out that nobody—including the three of us—came into the fellowship hall after your sermon to talk about it."

Ann jumped back in. "'Wait a minute!' I shouted at him. 'Steve's one mistake was making the announcement as a part of the sermon. We had no advance warning, and all of us had other plans that couldn't be canceled that day.'"

Arnie leaned forward in his chair, cleared his voice, and took his turn. "If what he had said about the sermon weren't enough, then he went off on this theory that, as far as he was concerned, it may have led to Flora's death because he thought she bought into your challenge. Ann gave him what-for about that, telling him Flora defended those children because of who she was and not because it had to do with anything you said."

Taking a breath, Arnie continued. "Stoner ignored our protests and plunged on with his accusations, saying that we have had a great thing going here at Incarnation with everyone in the community looking up to us. He contends that following your lead is going to lose us members and the respect of this community."

Jayne and I sat silently, brows wrinkled and frowning, paying rapt attention to our visitors.

Arnie waved his hands and continued the story. "At that point, Clifton came to his second complaint about you as pastor, and that was for having the burial service for Tyler Wooten. He claims that's not only an offense against our church but against Belvedere itself. As the leadership of Incarnation, it was therefore our responsibility to straighten things out. He threatened that, otherwise, the wrath of this community would come down on us like a ton of bricks. Straightening things out meant getting rid of you as our pastor."

Ann jumped in. "The thing that galled us the most was that Stoner was able to speak with confidence about the position he was taking because he already knew that the three board members who sat there like dumb bunnies were already solidly in agreement with him. With his vote, he was assured of getting his way, four to three, regardless of what we thought. That didn't end the discussion, though.

"We told them you are a great pastor who wants to lead us toward growth in Christ, to *be Christ* to the world around us. Though that may seem like a big step, it's the right step.

"Clifton gave us some malarkey about your sermon not meaning anything to those, like him, who live in the *real world*, and we responded with, what is the Christian faith all about if it's not being Christ's people in our *real world?*"

Paul wrung his hands and took a deep breath. "What's more, we told them, you're going to split the church if you ask Steve to resign. Not only are there those of us who believe he is taking us in exactly the right direction, but he is also highly respected in the community. Why the big thing of Steve having the funeral service for the Wooten kid? Why was he asked to do it? I'll bet it was because he's the clergyman most people in this town expect to do the right thing in a difficult situation.

"Of course that just set Stoner off again, saying, how could I call that the right thing, pointing out that the funeral parlor could have conducted the service. And so the argument went, back and forth, largely between Stoner and the three of us. But, in the end, there was the four-to-three vote."

Jayne, still trying to process the callousness of the decision, asked the group, "Is there no appeal to the decision—just thirty days and we're out?"

Arnie got up from his chair and began pacing. "There was no reasoning with Clifton and the others on the board, but we may be able to mount support from within the congregation to put a stop to this. Steve, you've got a lot of support in the congregation, and it's among those people who are serious about their faith in Christ. We'll be praying and thinking."

Ann nodded her head enthusiastically. "Arnie's right. Now it's time for us to be Christ to you."

In the midst of desperation, I had a moment of inspiration. "You're right. We say we believe in the power of prayer and that we are to be Christ to one another, and now is the time for it. Let's have an old-fashioned prayer meeting."

The five of us arranged our chairs in a circle facing each other, and I led off: "Lord, we're in need of a miracle right now. There's more going on than we can handle, but You can handle it. Please, Lord, step into this situation and bring peace, understanding, and harmony."

My prayer got the ball rolling, and we prayed for about an hour. There were heartfelt prayers from everybody, including Hannah. She had slipped into the room when she saw us praying and hopped into Jayne's lap, with Skeeter in her lap. She spoke in a soft, quivering voice. "Whatever happens, Lord, may we keep Skeeter."

Chapter 32

When the prayer meeting was over and the others had gone, I pulled Jayne aside. "Hannah's prayer broke my heart. How are the children reacting to all of this?"

"I don't think they know how to react. Even though Hannah probably didn't pick up on why Arnie, Ann, and Paul were here, and Brandon doesn't know about the call from Clifton, it should be clear to them that your position at Incarnation is in jeopardy. They don't want to admit it's true. They can't believe this is happening. They're conscious of how highly people think of you at Incarnation, but they don't know anything about church politics."

I wanted to go talk to them, but I had something else I had to do, and I hadn't even decided how to handle it with Jayne. So I didn't tell her the whole truth.

"Can you let me have a few hours to myself to try to get my mind around all that is happening and what's getting ready to happen? I know I haven't been here for you and the children as much as I should have in this crisis situation, but there are just some things I've got to work through. I don't even feel like supper, just not hungry. Can you forgive me?"

Jayne gave me *that look*. It's a half-smile below a wrinkled brow. It means "I'm married to a pastor."

I kissed her, grabbed my coat, and headed for the truck.

It was just getting dark out, and I actually felt a little hungry. I stopped at a drive-through, got a hamburger and lots of coffee, and headed for Sunnyside Trailer Park.

For obvious reasons, I was more attentive to my surroundings than I had been in my earlier visits to the trailer park. Now I was on reconnaissance, a guy on a mission to scout out the neighborhood and protect the innocent. A gravel road led off a paved city street into the entrance to the area. At the entrance sat a yellow and green Sunnyside Trailer Park sign, much faded with age and covered with dust from the road. The trailer homes varied in size and color, although all of them showed their age. Surprisingly, they were situated on lots somewhat larger than our neighborhood. The land was, of course, much less expensive. So, what these people lacked in the niceties that the more affluent neighborhoods had was offset by the additional yard space. Some of Connie's neighbors used that space for home vegetable gardens, but most of the yards were overgrown in weeds.

The gravel road continued through the trailer park, rutted in some places and mainly dirt rather than gravel in others. Very few streetlights dotted the area. There were virtually no trees.

Connie's house was the first on my right as I drove into the park. It sat about a hundred feet off the road, and there was considerable distance between her and her nearest neighbors. Some of the trailers had small porches on the front, but not Connie's.

After driving through the area, I doubled back and out the entrance. Turning my truck around, I pulled off the left side of the road among some scraggly trees. I knew my fire-engine red Dodge Dakota wouldn't be as obvious in the nighttime as it was in daylight.

Although I parked outside the trailer park, I had a decent view of Connie's house. I thought I was well prepared to spot any troublemakers who might come into the area and threaten Connie. I also thought I wouldn't be too conspicuous to inquiring eyes. So I settled down, ate my meal, and waited to see what might happen.

Coward that I am, I was filled with anxiety. What if Mike Troutman and others actually showed up? What would I do? Make some phone calls? I had Philip Treadway at the top of my list. Also Arnie Dixon and Paul

Rivers. And *Clifton Stoner*. Stoner, in spite of everything else, was probably the most influential person in the area, and I didn't believe he would condone violent action, even against Connie Wooten.

As I waited, it seemed time for shaping my thoughts into prayers. I first prayed for myself and for Connie that nothing bad would happen that night. Then I prayed about the larger situation I faced.

"Lord, it may well be that it's time for us to leave Belvedere. We've had a good life here and, I believe, a good ministry. You know I think I heard Your call to tell these good folks about the incarnation challenge I believe You had laid on me on behalf of them. . .and myself. Everything seems to have gone wrong since then, but You did not cause what has happened. The people of Incarnation Church and the people of this community are good-hearted people, but as You said in Jeremiah, the heart can be deceitful above all things."

The weight of my own words brought into focus the bleak future that seemed to be ahead for me and my family because of what seemed like deceitful hearts.

I continued. "Forgive me, Lord, if I am judging Clifton Stoner and others on the board. They think they are doing the right thing, but I believe they are being deceived. Give them a heart to know You, as you also said in Jeremiah, and a new heart, as You said in Ezekiel.

"And Holy Father, I ask You for protection for Connie Wooten. She has given herself to You, but she is filled with pain and doubt and real fear. Give her peace, and show her the way You have for her."

Having laid myself bare before the Lord in my prayers, I had to admit my concern for Jayne, Brandon, and Hannah—and our future—remained paramount as well. "Protect my little family, Lord, and show us what You have in store for us. We want to be in Your will. We want to be Christ to the world around us."

That wasn't the end of my praying or my thinking, but I knew I had to focus on what might happen in the hours of darkness ahead. The sound of car tires on gravel heightened my anxiety. Every time a car drove by, my heartbeat increased rapidly. Finally, traffic into the trailer park ended, but when there wasn't any noise, the quietness brought its own terror. After all, if terror was afoot, wouldn't it come quietly?

So I sat there for hours, as though awaiting impending doom, playing games in my mind about what I would do and how I would do it. I considered various scenarios, and my imagination took me down some strange pathways. Part of the problem was that I had never had any idea of doing to someone what these guys might have in mind for

Connie. It was all out of my range of experience, but that didn't stop me from coming up with all sorts of evil plots and then trying to decide what I would do to deal with each of them.

It was a nerve-wracking night and left me edgy and even more exhausted than I already was from the events of the day.

Fortunately for me, nothing happened. The night remained quiet and still. The lights in Connie Wooten's trailer had gone out long before I left at two in the morning.

Chapter 33

Saturday, October 21

I lay in bed late Saturday morning, groggy from too little sleep. Even after getting home in the wee hours of the morning, I still had too much on my mind. My thoughtful wife brought me coffee as soon as she heard me stirring.

She arched an eyebrow. "That must have been some session you had with the Lord last night." I had a feeling she had found me out. I always had that feeling about Jayne. So, propped up in bed and looking up at her, I took a life-saving sip of coffee, let it begin to have its effect, and confessed.

"I didn't want to worry you about last night. Philip Treadway and I made a pact to keep an eye on Connie Wooten's trailer for a couple of nights, hoping this thing will blow over. Last night was my night."

"What?" Jayne looked at me as though she saw a stranger. "What happened?"

"Nothing. All was quiet, and I did have a lot of time for thinking and praying."

She shook her head. "I don't like this. You've had no training in handling violence. You're supposed to counsel and comfort those who are facing disappointment and danger, not get in the middle of it."

I rubbed my forehead. "I don't see myself getting into a dangerous situation. Philip and I are thinking that one of us being there would keep the bad guys from doing anything. They won't want to be caught doing whatever they have in mind." I tried to say these things as though I really believed them, but I was far from sure that I did. Who knows what these guys might do?

"You don't sound very convincing." A frown of deep concern came on her face. She sat on the edge of the bed.

I scooted over for her. "The plan is that if either of us sees that something is about to happen, we call in reinforcements. Neither of us plans to be a hero." Again, I was feeling something very different within myself from the story I was trying to sell Jayne. And of course, she didn't buy it.

Between gritted teeth, she looked me straight in the eyes and said, "You've got to get her police protection."

"I've tried, and it didn't work. The police chief is the uncle of the ringleader of this trouble, and he wants Connie gone from Belvedere as much as the nephew does. Philip and I will be careful. We know our limitations.

"Besides, for me it was just last night and it's over. Today I have the awkward challenge of preparing a sermon for tomorrow. Will the service begin with an announcement that we are leaving, and what kind of an announcement will it be? That's my panic of the day."

"You make that sound almost as dangerous as your guard duty last night."

"Kinda feels like it." I gave her a half-smile and took another sip of coffee.

When I got to the office, Betty Ferguson, who always came in on Saturday mornings, sat at her desk with a red nose and weepy eyes. "I can't believe you're leaving. What are we going to do without you?"

"Probably find someone better." I shrugged, trying to make light of the situation. But there was no consoling her. "How did you find out?"

"Ann Boronski called me. She's devastated."

"I know. She and others came by and prayed with us yesterday evening."

"You're going to fight this, aren't you?" A determined look grew on her face. "Surely you aren't going to cave in and abandon all of us who think you're the best thing that ever happened to this church. Clifton Stoner has done a lot for Incarnation, but he has no right to dictate who will be our spiritual leader, and we both know that he's the one who's behind this. You've been here fifteen years. If you leave like this, it will split this church wide open."

Betty was going full steam now, and there was no stopping her.

I shifted my stance. "What are you suggesting?"

"We could mount a phone and e-mail campaign. Not you, but those of us who don't want you to leave. The phone here is going to be ringing soon enough. Things like this can't be kept quiet in a town like Belvedere."

I had grave misgivings about starting a fight within the church. It was Saturday morning, and nothing would be official until tomorrow.

"Let's wait. Maybe things will remain quiet today. Let's just put this in the Lord's hands and see what happens. If there is no uproar about the announcement tomorrow, it may mean that my time here should come to an end."

She pounded the desk. "That's not going to happen. I'll start my own uproar if no one else does!"

I held a hand up to calm her. "I'll put it another way. You're an employee of the church, not an employee of mine. You owe it to the elected authorities of the church to be loyal in your role as secretary. Put your personal views aside today. As to phone calls and e-mails and such, respond that Clifton Stoner is the chairman of the board of the church and you have heard nothing from him. Plead ignorance. After today what you do is up to you. But again, I would caution you not to take steps that could split the church."

She didn't like that advice, but she ultimately seemed to accept it.

With that crisis behind me, I sat at my desk coming to grips with a sermon. However, my first priority was to call Philip Treadway and report to him on my Friday night adventure, or lack thereof, at Sunnyside Trailer Park. He took it all matter-of-factly and promised to be on patrol that evening. He said he had talked with the sheriff, who was disgusted with Clyde Matthews's apparent inaction in the situation. He said he'd get in touch with the state folks to see what they think we should do and assured me that his guys were available if needed.

With that taken care of, I plunged into the unknown by way of my sermon preparation. I decided, after prayer, to use the Scriptures normally appointed for that Sunday and preach on them just as though it were any other Sunday. Fortunately, I was able to get caught up in my work suffi-ciently to put my other problems behind me.

Chapter 34

Saturday evening started out on a peaceful note. We had family supper together and avoided talking about the crisis we faced.

After the meal, Brandon watched television and Hannah walked Skeeter then joined Brandon in the family room. Jayne and I sat at the kitchen table while I told her how I planned to handle the sermon. In the back of my mind, however, loomed Philip Treadway. *Is he at the trailer park? Is anything happening there? Will I be getting a telephone call?*

It had been dark outside for perhaps an hour when the phone rang.

Philip, panic in his voice. "Better get here, and get here fast. I couldn't get away from the store when I wanted to and have just gotten here. All hell is breaking loose. They plan to burn her out, and things have already started."

I grabbed my jacket and headed for the front door with

no explanation to Jayne and the children but that I had an emergency.

Even children can sense moments of panic. Brandon and Hannah realized something was wrong when the call came on my cell phone, jumped from where they were sitting, and began to pound me with questions.

"What's wrong?" Hannah pleaded.

"Can't talk. Got to go."

"Dad, let me come with you." Brandon's voice sounded firm, but his eyes begged like a child's.

"No way, son."

"Please." He desperately grabbed my arm.

"No, no, *no!*" I shouted as I jerked myself away from him and ran to the truck.

My last sight before speeding away was my son, so seemingly unconcerned about anyone other than himself, slumped in defeat at the door because his father would not let him share in a crisis he didn't understand but in which he sincerely wanted to help.

As I drove, I placed my calls, including the one to Clifton Stoner.

"Clifton, it's Steve Long. I know how you feel about Connie Wooten, but a gang of hotheads is ready to burn her out of her trailer, whether she stays in it or not. You're the only person in town they will listen to. Please come."

"I'll be there." Surprisingly, Stoner's reply sounded subdued.

Approaching the trailer park a few minutes later, I saw Philip had parked on the road just outside the entrance and was standing by his car. I pulled in behind him. Before I could get out of the truck, Philip hurried to meet me. Connie Wooten stood in horror at her front door, staring at her tormentors, who had lit torches and waved them in the air.

Philip briefed me on what had happened. "It's Mike Troutman and some of his goons. They've splashed the front of the Wooten trailer with gasoline and have tried to talk her into leaving, telling her they are going to burn her house down. She has said she can't leave because there is no place for her to go. She pleaded with them to leave her alone. They've just lit their torches."

"What do we do?" I tried to steady my voice though my body trembled—whether from fear or fury I wasn't quite sure.

Philip sighed deeply. "Wait until we have some help and hope nothing happens in the meantime. I've made my phone calls, including to the sheriff, Don Jones, but it will take him or his guys some time to get here from Davisville."

Though I was furious, I was frankly scared stiff. Several

owners of trailers surrounding Connie's huddled at their front doors or wandered out toward the road, but they were clearly afraid to do anything themselves. I guess they could see how easy it would be for their trailers to be set on fire as well.

The smell of gasoline filled the air. One toss of a torch and Connie's trailer could go up in flames. Fortunately, Mike Troutman's crowd wanted to scare Connie out of the trailer before torching it. But they were filled with beer and bloodlust, and anything could happen in a moment.

"Get out of there, you stupid woman, before we burn you up in that pile of trash where you live."

"You're the bride of Satan, and we don't need your kind around here."

"You've caused us enough trouble. We don't want you in our town. We don't ever want to see you again."

"Burn, baby, burn," one wild-eyed drunk shouted.

The threats continued for several minutes as Troutman's gang swung their torches back and forth in the air, some of them with a torch in one hand and a bottle of beer in the other. In a shaky, pleading voice, Connie Wooten stood her ground. "Where do you expect me to go?" Her voice began to crack, though. "I'd leave if I could. Please go away and leave me alone."

My heart broke for this poor woman. She had lost everything except her meager trailer home, and now they were threatening to take even that from her. Worse still, in a reckless moment she could lose not only her home but her life.

I wanted to do something. I *had* to do something. Why me? I was the weakest limb on the tree. Where were the police? I knew the answer to that. Where was the volunteer fire department? We had forgotten to put them on the call list. Where was anyone but me to step into this situation and do something?

"As the Father has sent Me, I also send you."

It was like an out-of-body experience. I couldn't believe I was the one who suddenly ran into Connie's front yard. It was like I watched someone else do it. But I heard myself shout at Troutman and his cohorts, "Stop, guys! This is the wrong thing to do. If you kill this woman, you'll have murder on your hands. Walk away from this and it's over. Go ahead with it and you'll spend the rest of your lives in prison."

But by this time they were drunk with power. One of them apparently recognized me. "Get out of the way, preacher, or we'll burn your butt along with hers."

Then it happened. A torch sailed through the air. As if in slow motion, I watched it arc toward the trailer. Thrown with hate-filled force, the burning torch bounced off the trailer onto the ground. But of course the ground had been saturated with gasoline.

As I think back on it, I don't know how I did it. But the voice in my head repeated, *"As the Father has sent Me, I also send you."* I ran, pulling my jacket off as I went. I arrived the moment the torch landed, threw my jacket over it, and stamped the fire out. Thank goodness the gas had not soaked the ground at that point.

With a withering look at the guy who had thrown the torch, I immediately headed to the front door of Connie's trailer, as Philip Treadway flanked me. We pushed our way into the trailer, and then I turned and shouted, "Have some sense, guys. If you toss any of those torches, you are going to kill three people. That's first-degree murder, and you all will be guilty."

Philip coughed the words, "What are we doing, Steve? Those guys have been drinking and have mayhem on their minds. . .if they have any minds. Just one more senseless toss of a torch and we're dead."

"If they're stupid enough to kill Connie, she isn't going to die alone," I boasted, more bluff than bravery.

Connie pleaded with us, "You don't need to do this."

But I knew I did and tried to silence her. As I looked out at Mike Troutman and his buddies, I detected murder still burned in their eyes. But I could also see cars coming into the trailer park in significant numbers. I prayed they were the ones Philip and I had called and not more troublemakers.

The rage among the men seemed to increase rather than dissipate, either from the frustration of meeting opposition or too much drink. For a few moments, they were in a strange ebb and flow dance of death. They would say things to one another like, "We'd better get out of here while we can," and start backing away and then contradict that with, "We came here to do a job—let's do it," and move back toward the trailer. In the course of this erratic behavior, their threats increased.

"If you're fool enough to stand by that witch, you deserve to burn with her," one of the men shouted as they moved dangerously close to the fuel-soaked building, still waving their torches in the air.

In truth, although I had talked big about dying with Connie, if they threw the torches, my real plan was for us to scramble out of the trailer once flames headed our way. But even that was an iffy proposition, and I hoped it wouldn't come to it. But who were these people arriving in a caravan of cars?

Several got out of their cars and surged toward the scene, Clifton Stoner in the lead. Boldly, he stepped between the torchbearers and the trailer and shouted, "Men, you know who I am and that I lost my wife in that shooting. I know how you feel. But what you're doing won't solve anything. Douse those torches and go home. This woman's got enough of a burden to carry the rest of her life."

"Get out of there, Mr. Stoner." Mike Troutman hurled the words at him defiantly. "You don't need to be a part of this."

"But I am." Stoner moved to the front door of the trailer. "You kill these people and you kill me, too."

While all of this played out, a continuing parade of vehicles swarmed into the trailer park, and more people spilled out of them and ran toward the chaotic scene at the Wooten trailer.

If I wasn't scared enough, this mad rush of so many others into the picture only heightened my fear. When mob rule takes over, anything can happen.

But this mob did not shout vengeance. Miraculously, they were not shouting at all!

These were not hotheads. These were the good people of Incarnation Church and other residents of Belvedere, and all of a sudden they surrounded Connie Wooten's home as a protective barrier.

With a sheepish grin, Clifton Stoner turned to us. "I made a few phone calls on my way here."

And as people around here say, "Bless their hearts,

someone finally thought to call the volunteer fire department." We could hear the fire engines blaring and the flashing lights of sheriff's deputies.

Troutman and his gang doused their torches and ran stumbling away.

An epidemic of tears, hugs, and shouts broke out among the assembled crowd. They had each played a part in averting a major disaster, and they celebrated triumphantly. They were in no hurry to leave.

Meanwhile, Connie Wooten was in the embarrassing predicament of being a sort of celebrity instead of public enemy number one. Several people from the crowd edged up to her front door to wish her well. Even Clifton Stoner mumbled some words of encouragement before accepting her thanks and prying himself away from the house to slip away.

Over his shoulder, Clifton called to me, "Come by my home when you leave here, no matter how late."

Connie was especially grateful to Philip and me for taking our stand with her at the trailer door. She appeared, however, both emotionally and physically drained. I eased her back into the room, got her seated at the breakfast table, and under her guidance, brewed some coffee. Philip sat with her as they relived what happened.

As the crowd began to dissipate, I went out and talked

with the firemen. It didn't take any encouragement from me for them to see what needed to be done. As best they could, they used their hoses to dilute the gasoline along the front of the trailer and sprayed the front of the trailer itself. Then some of the firemen, with consent from Connie, went into the backyard and hauled shovels full of dirt to spread around the front base of the house because there was no way to completely eliminate the presence and smell of the fuel.

One fireman mentioned that he had found a jacket that appeared to have been used to snuff out a torch. I didn't tell him it was mine.

"It was totally ruined, of course," he said as he held it up, demonstrating the obvious.

I gave him a slight grin. "Thank God that it was the only victim tonight."

The sheriff's deputies were busy talking with those still present, hearing the story of what had happened, and trying to get as many names of the perpetrators as they could. They questioned Connie at some length but with consideration for what she had been through. They, and we, made sure Connie was taken care of for the evening. Fred and Rosa, neighbors, insisted that if Connie did not come spend the night with them, they would stay with her.

When Philip and I left around midnight, everything was quiet and peaceful.

When we parted, I became a little emotional—almost in tears—as I thanked Philip once again for all his help and support. "You're a real friend. I've never known anyone as totally reliable as you are, and I'm very grateful."

"Same here," was the warm response.

Chapter 35

I made a quick call to Jayne that the crisis was over but I was headed to Clifton Stoner's at his request. As I drove, I gave her an abbreviated sketch of what happened at the trailer park and Stoner's surprising part in it.

Clifton met me at the door when I arrived at his home. He had a wry grin on his face and immediately extended his hand in a friendly handshake.

As soon as we were seated in his huge living room, he told me an amazing story.

He settled back in his chair and crossed his arms. "I know it's late, but relax. This will take some time, but I promise it will be worth it."

He slipped his hands to his lap and looked down at them. "Following the meeting with the church board here yesterday, I sat down to a meal Helen had fixed me. You may know she is a superb cook. There I sat in my big, beautiful dining room, roast beef cooked just the way I like it. The wonderful smell of food filled the room, but I just wasn't hungry."

Clifton adjusted himself in his chair and looked up at me. "*Why?* I wondered. Well, of course, the loss of Flora left me heartbroken and completely drained emotionally. But there was something more troubling me. Shouldn't I have felt good about resolving my conflict with you? I was sure we were justified in the action we had taken."

With a sheepish grin on his face, he said, "I almost enjoyed calling you to tell you that you were through at Incarnation Church. Enough of your pushing the church too far! Enough of your entangling the church in the whole Wooten affair! Good riddance. But something niggled at my heartstrings and left me uneasy."

I tried not to be fidgety in my chair. Clifton took a deep breath and continued. "After eating only a few bites of supper and making excuses to Helen, I went into the family room and tried to read. After she had cleaned up and left for the evening, I turned on the television but found nothing of interest. I wandered around the empty house, looked painfully at items that reminded me of Flora, and finally forced myself to bed, taking a book with me. When the book kept falling from my hands, I gave up, turned out the light, and went to sleep.

"*It's just part of the aging process*, I thought to myself

when I awoke in the middle of the night. It had been happening for some time. Even before Flora's death, I would go to sleep without too much trouble but then wake up, wide awake, in the early hours of the morning. I would be flooded with concerns about work or personal matters. Now it was always about Flora."

I wondered where all of this was going and tried not to look at my watch but to stay focused on what he told me.

Clifton shook his head, frowning and looking down in sadness. "Flora, Flora, Flora," he moaned. "I miss her so much. Not only did I love her, but she kept me in line, from going off on tangents, focused. She loved me when I was unlovable. How can I go on without her?" Grief tore at his heart, and his eyes became wet with tears.

He raised his hands, palms up. "Sorry."

It was time for me to break the ice. "No need to apologize for talking about Flora. She was an exceptional woman, and I know how much you loved one another."

Clifton shook his head slightly, as though gathering his thoughts. "It was like I was talking with Flora. Then I thought about her spirituality, her faithfulness to God. She was much deeper into that than I am. You know that. The next thing I knew, I was talking to God."

He looked up at me as if seeking affirmation, and I nodded.

He continued, "It was as though God was showing me that it wasn't anything you said that got Flora killed. It was just Flora being herself. I wanted to blame you for her death, and God wasn't having any of it. I never considered these middle-of-the-night episodes as times for prayer, but that was what happened. Suddenly I found myself asking, *Lord, did I do the right thing in getting our pastor fired?*"

Clifton took a deep breath and shook his head again. "Strangely, what immediately came to me was a conversation I had shortly after becoming chairman of the board at Incarnation Church. I ran into an old friend, a college fraternity brother, on a business trip. As we tried to catch up on what was happening in our lives, I mentioned I had become the board chairman at my church and was still trying to figure out how to function most effectively."

Wondering where all of this was going, I again tried not to squirm in my chair.

Not pausing a moment, Clifton continued, "I pointed out that I ran a successful bank and tried to run the church in the same way. I wanted to keep the members happy so they'd keep attending and giving, and I saw myself as the guy primarily responsible for seeing that everything was done in good order.

"My friend smiled and said, 'That's exactly how I saw

things when I became senior warden of the vestry of our Anglican Church. I wanted to keep things in order. Then an interesting thing happened. The church agreed to have a renewal weekend. It was one of these things where a group of people come from other churches to talk about unique experiences they have had with the Lord, how they found the Lord, or how the Lord healed them from anything from addictions to physical illnesses. They were called witnesses, and they were to witness to God in their lives. This felt scary to me, so I made sure I was included in all the planning, and I attended every session of the event. I wanted to be in control. I wanted to make absolutely sure things didn't get out of hand and shoot the church off on some weird tangent.'"

Clifton grinned. "This guy talked my language, or at least so I thought. Because then he looked directly at me and said, 'But guess what happened? I was the guy who ended up getting renewed! It completely changed my life. I started a men's Bible study group and volunteered to be a witness at these renewal weekends in other churches.'

"Dumbfounded by that remark, I didn't want to hear any more. It turned out we were interrupted, and I didn't have to endure the embarrassment of listening to that diatribe. But last night, that incident all of a sudden spoke to me. My problem is that I want to control the church just like I do the bank! I haven't been open to what God might have to say."

My inner self was shouting *Hallelujah!*, but I looked intently at Clifton in anticipation of what came next.

He gave me a half-smile, palms up. "Do I need to say it? God had broken through to me. I was immediately convicted of my grievous injustice against you. All of a sudden I felt very guilty for what I had done. I asked God's forgiveness, and now I am asking yours."

There were tears in my eyes, and I had no words. I got up, and he did likewise. I gave him a bear hug and got one in return.

Jayne stayed up until I got home. If anxiety and relief can be reflected on a person's face at the same time, that was Jayne's. She was so glad to see me but wondered about the details of what I had been through. We stood hugging one another at the front door until anxiety faded and relief took over for both of us. It was then that I related everything that had happened, including the visit with Clifton Stoner.

Jayne's practical mind kicked in at that point. "I wonder what this means for us."

I gave her a wry grin. "Well, I guess we'll just have to wait and see."

New anxiety surfaced for me, however, as I remembered the incident with Brandon as I was leaving. The solid wall between us had shown a slight crack when he asked to go with me, but there was no way I could have allowed him to be in the middle of the danger I anticipated. Did my negative reaction reseal the crack?

"How did Brandon react when I left?" I managed to squeeze the question out of my mouth, fearing the answer.

Jayne frowned. "I wish I could tell you he is okay, but he's not. If anything, what was bad between you is now worse. When you had gone, he stormed through the room and shouted, 'I'm almost fifteen years old and he treats me like a baby. . .when he pays any attention to me at all!' He went to his room and slammed the door so hard it seemed to make the house shake."

Too late to do anything about it tonight, I said to myself. Just when it looked like things might work out for us at Incarnation, I couldn't seem to work things out with my own son. For now that seemed to be the more important issue.

Chapter 36

Sunday, October 22

That Sunday morning broke bright and beautiful in Belvedere, with crisp air and vibrant fall colors. I was in a state of exultation because of what had happened Saturday night but in desperation concerning my relationship with my son.

While Jayne and I sipped our early morning mugs of coffee, Clifton Stoner called. The message was short and sweet. Very matter-of-factly he said, "Steve, Clifton. The mistake of firing you will be rectified at an early morning board meeting today. See you at church." I only had time for a quick thank-you before he hung up.

From the conversation with Clifton the night before, I wasn't overly surprised, but I was elated. I fell on my knees and thanked God. Jayne realized what had happened and dropped to the floor beside me. I wanted to call the kids into the room to give them the news but realized I had to revise my sermon, with limited time to do it. So, once again realizing I was putting time with Brandon on the back burner, I quickly dressed and headed to church.

For Incarnation Church, it was, by any measure, a remarkable day. By the time worship began, the church was packed. There were a number of first-time visitors. Smiles and happy greetings resounded across the sanctuary because some members of the congregation now had a new relationship with one another as a result of standing in solidarity at Connie Wooten's trailer the night before.

In advance of the worship service, the hurriedly called board meeting reinstated me as pastor by a unanimous vote, followed with a written apology and a raise in salary. Paul Rivers brought me the news, relieving Clifton Stoner of an awkward encounter.

I based my sermon on Matthew 16:24–26, about Christian discipleship, and John 15:12, Jesus' command to love one another. I began it as though nothing special had happened the night before.

"God can orchestrate marvelous things out of the worst of tragedies. There is no better example than the crucifixion and resurrection of our Lord and Savior Jesus Christ.

"When He died on the cross, it seemed that the greatest hope of mankind had died with Him. The long-awaited Messiah, the Son of God, had perished in humiliation and defeat. At least, so it appeared.

"But God had something else in mind; and what happened on that Friday was completely reversed on the following Sunday. What we call Good Friday became Easter Day. What seemed to be the end of all things became the beginning of all things.

"Last Sunday I challenged you. God incarnate came to our world in His Son Jesus Christ. When Jesus was no longer here on earth, that incarnation continued through Christ's people. . .those of us who call ourselves Christians. When God could no longer be present to us in His Son, He sent the Holy Spirit, who empowers us to be Christ to the world around us.

"We've had a chance over these last few days to see what that might look like. We saw it in Flora Stoner, who gave her life to protect students at Belvedere High. We saw it in Clifton Stoner, who faced down a murderous mob to protect the life and property of Connie Wooten last night. We saw it in the courage of the people of Belvedere—including many of you—who supported Clifton by standing with him against the attack on Mrs. Wooten. And today, as a result of the love of Christ among us, perhaps we feel a little better about ourselves, about Belvedere, and about Incarnation Church."

There was a sudden outburst of applause in spite of the normally subdued behavior of the people of Incarnation

Church. Some people actually high-fived each other in the pews.

My eyes moistened with tears. After the noise died down, I continued. "As wonderful as all of this is, it is only a start. We are all called to be Christ to the world around us, but seldom will we have the opportunity to demonstrate that in such dramatic ways as those I've mentioned. It will be in the day-to-day loving and caring for others that occurs in the routines of our lives. When Jesus talked of carrying our crosses and laying down our lives for others, He knew that we would be doing it more in the simple things of life than in dramatic confrontations—though we would need to be prepared for those as well.

"So, today I give you again the incarnation challenge: be Christ to your world in whatever way God calls you. We are not just to try to imitate Christ by walking in His footsteps; we are to incarnate Christ, to be in His place in all aspects of our lives.

"In my sermons for the foreseeable future, I'll be exploring what all of that means. Amen? Amen."

Chapter 37

Getting away from the church that Sunday morning was difficult. Everyone seemed to be in a jovial mood as they chatted away with each other and with me. It was a mob scene as I greeted people at the sanctuary door at the end of the service. Some knew of my involvement at Connie's the night before or had been told by others.

"Way to go, Pastor," several people said.

"You made it sound like Mr. Stoner was the hero last night, but that's not the way it looked to me." A number of remarks were similar to that one.

"Glad it all worked out. We'd hate to lose you." The woman who said that left me puzzled. Was she talking about what happened at the trailer park, or had word gotten out of my having been fired?

So it went. As people headed out of church into the sunny autumn day, my spirits should have been soaring. Unfortunately, nagging at the back of my mind were the issues that would have to be faced with Brandon.

As soon as I could get away from the sanctuary, I began looking for Jayne and the children. They had come in the minivan, but I couldn't see it in the parking lot that still bustled with activity. I got in my truck and started home.

Jayne met me at the front door. "Where's Brandon?" she asked, a quiver in her voice and a questioning look on her face. "He said he'd wait and come home with you."

Failure on my part once again! This time I didn't think it was my fault. How was I to know that Brandon wanted to ride with me? I hadn't seen him. Now he would feel he had been intentionally abandoned or just forgotten. And where was he?

In a state of panic, I laid my hands on her shoulders. "I'll go back to church and look for him. You and Hannah stay here. Someone else may have given him a ride."

I broke the speed limit getting back to church, although traffic was light following worship services. And there was Brandon, sitting on the front steps of the church, hunched over and looking lost.

"Brandon," I shouted as I pulled up at the curb in front of him, "I'm sorry. I didn't know you were coming home with me."

With an accusing look, he slowly opened the door and slunk into the truck.

I continued to explain. "The car was gone when I got ready to leave, and I thought you were with your mom. I didn't see you."

"It's okay." He didn't sound as though it was.

That got my ire up. "Wait a minute." My voice hardened. "How was I to know? Do you think I intentionally went off without you?"

Brandon mumbled something, turned away from me, and looked out the side window.

Instead of driving home, I called Jayne on my cell phone and told her I had found Brandon and that we would be home in a little while. I told her not to hold lunch for us. We'd pick up something. She didn't argue with me, figuring I had something in mind—like the needed conversation with Brandon.

"Would you like to stop at the burger place and get some lunch?"

"Sure." He was wide-eyed and open-mouthed with surprise. I realized how seldom I had gone to a burger place just to have a meal with my son.

The place was crowded, so we each got burgers, fries, and sweet tea to go and drove to that spot on the outskirts of Belvedere where I had gone to ponder why Otis Huntington had killed himself. It was my thinking place, and I wanted to share it with Brandon.

We sat in the truck eating our burgers on that hill that is the highest place in the area, looking out on the town far below us. Brandon's countenance changed. He seemed to be enjoying himself, polishing off his first hamburger in record time. Why had it taken me so long to share a moment like this with my son?

I took a big swallow of sweet tea to bolster my courage to start this long-needed conversation. "This is where I come when I'm trying to sort through things in my life, and it's a joy to be doing it with you today."

"What are you trying to sort through today?"

"You."

He half-turned to me but didn't look me in the eyes. "What do you mean?"

"I'm trying to figure out why I have so much trouble communicating with you. I love you, you know."

Then came the incredible breakthrough. His Adam's apple bobbled. "I know you do, Dad. That's why you wouldn't let me go with you last night. You knew you were going into a dangerous situation."

I was astonished. I wanted to grab him and hug him but felt that wouldn't have been appropriate right then.

"You're right. I was scared stiff, and if I wasn't sure I could take care of myself, I certainly wouldn't have been able to take care of both of us."

"Tell me about it." His voice softened as though he really meant it.

So I did. I gave him all the details without trying to make my role out as anything special.

"Dad, the word is that you were the real hero last night, and I'm proud of you."

By that time we had finished with our meal, and I did lean over and give him a long and firm hug, one in which he hugged back at least equally.

"I'm sorry I have always seemed too busy or distracted to have the time with you I want to. I know it's hard being a preacher's kid. You probably feel that everyone is looking at you expecting you to be superspiritual just because you're from a clergy family. Yet, in truth, you have a father who is so involved in the lives of others that he has little time for his own family. It's tough on your mother, too, but she more or less knew what she was getting into. You and Hannah didn't have that choice.

"And then you have to put up with what people say about me," I continued. "People being what they are, it's often criticism that you probably hear. That's why I want to have a new relationship with you. I want to find time for us to be together, go fishing or whatever you'd like to do. Most of all, just time to talk things through."

"I'd like that." Brandon nodded his head and smiled.

And then he unloaded. He told me the problems he dealt with in his world, was honest about the resentments he had held because I hadn't seemed to care about him, and gave me a glimpse into his dreams.

I don't want to get maudlin by talking about how that made me feel, but I melted into a bucket of tears when he finished. Fortunately, he cried with me.

Chapter 38

The midweek edition of the *Belvedere Herald* featured what had happened at Connie Wooten's on Saturday night. Charles Barnett had changed the normal format for the first page. It contained his own news article about the episode, plus an editorial he had also written and placed—unusual for such a feature—in the center of the front page.

The news article covered what had occurred at the Sunnyside Trailer Park in considerable detail, including the names of the men who had assaulted her house and threatened her life, and the men who had come to her rescue. It concluded by telling of the volunteer fire department spraying down Mrs. Wooten's home with water to wash away the gasoline as best they could. And this is what the editorial said:

Night of Terror, Night of Glory
This past week had been tragic enough. But that

wasn't enough for some. Not content that young Tyler Wooten—the cause of the tragedy—was dead, a handful of men wanted revenge against his mother and attempted to burn her out of her home Saturday night. Despite having been warned about threats against Mrs. Wooten, our "valiant" police chief, Clyde Matthews, did nothing to prevent the situation.

Connie Wooten is not someone for us to hate. She has lost her only child, having just recently lost her husband to cancer. She is a good person and was a hard worker at the Belvedere Motel until she was fired for no other reason than pressure put on the motel by those who apparently *do* hate. She was not the cause of her son's demented outburst, though she undoubtedly is in great pain because of what he did. She is someone toward whom we should have sympathy, not animosity.

But there were troublemakers who felt otherwise, and they would have their revenge at any cost. They showed up with gasoline and torches. The fuel was splashed on the trailer where Connie Wooten lives, and these "stalwart vigilantes" were ready to set fire to the house even though Mrs. Wooten would not leave.

The catastrophe did not happen, however. Steve Long, pastor of Incarnation Church, along with Clifton Stoner and Philip Treadway, leading lights in our community for many years, stood at the door of the Wooten home and defied the attackers, pledging to die with Mrs. Wooten if the attackers were insane enough to torch the place.

But that was only part of the miracle. Somehow word of what unfolded in the trailer park began to reach an increasing number of citizens of our fair city, and large numbers made their way to this turbulent scene. But contrary to human nature, instead of standing around gawking at what was happening, they became a part of it—and a very positive part indeed!

The proud and fair-minded people of Belvedere swarmed around Mrs. Wooten's humble abode as an additional ring of protection, defying the intentions of those who would have burned her out. They were people from all walks of life, including some who had lost loved ones in the shooting, showing their goodwill in clear opposition to blind hate.

Yet conspicuous in their absence were those charged with protecting *all* of our people—the

Belvedere police force, which we later learned had been forbidden from protecting Connie Wooten by Police Chief Clyde Matthews.

A night of terror became a night of glory. Congratulations to the people of Belvedere for demonstrating both compassion and bravery. But to Chief Matthews and that handful of rabble-rousers who sought to murder an innocent woman, you are the ones we could do without.

Chapter 39

Sunday, October 29

Clouds blotted out the sun, and the breeze felt chilly for northern Georgia in late October, but the weather didn't dampen my mood. I arose early and was on my second cup of coffee by the time Jayne came into the kitchen.

"Well, you're bright-eyed and bushy-tailed this gloomy day." She appeared with straggly hair and sleepy eyes, though, as far as I'm concerned, she is always beautiful.

"I don't think it's going to rain, and we should have a good turnout at worship. I'm looking forward to the day."

"What specifically?"

"The baptism of Connie Wooten, for one thing. And whether the enthusiasm we saw last Sunday and somewhat during the past week will spill over once again at the worship service, for another. And whether Philip Treadway will be in church, for yet another."

Jayne had a doubtful look on her face. "I hope you're not

going to be disappointed."

I gave her what I wanted to be a winning smile and said, "I don't think anything can disappoint me today."

Hannah appeared, dragging herself along only half awake, with Skeeter on his retractable leash. She mumbled, "Good morning," and headed for the door to walk her dog. I say *her* dog because that was one of the blessings of the past week. The church board had voted to suspend its own no-pets policy and let Hannah keep Skeeter.

I was keyed up for Brandon's arrival on the scene because I wanted to continue to develop this new relationship with him. His warm smile soon greeted us. He seemed like a new person when he came in and plunked down at the breakfast table in the kitchen. He looked as though he had something special to tell us.

"What's up?"

"Something I meant to tell you about. At youth church this morning we're going to be discussing how, as Christians, to do Halloween this year."

My theological mind immediately kicked in, and I wanted to point out to him that, in ancient days, what we call Halloween was actually a holy day: All Hallows' Eve. I would have then given him a short history lesson on how it got corrupted and a lot more information he didn't need. Fortunately, I held my tongue. "Tell us about it."

Brandon leaned forward on the table as though sharing with us the secrets of the kingdom. "Well, we're not telling the kids to quit doing trick or treat. But some of us older ones plan to accompany them. We're going to encourage them to wear costumes that aren't gory and not to look as though they are dangerous or plan to do bad things. And of course we're going to expect them to thank people for the candy they get."

"Sounds like a plan to me."

While Jayne nodded her head in agreement, she added, "Brandon, you're really to be commended for whatever part you have had in doing this. It sounds like some of these ideas may have been yours."

Brandon almost blushed. "Thanks. Maybe a little."

I got dressed and headed to church. As I looked into the sanctuary, the women had decorated it with fall colors of vibrant yellow, flaming red, and dark brown. The scene took my breath away. These women showed their devotion to God by the care with which they prepared for worship each Sunday and on other special occasions. Maybe it was time to acknowledge their ministry with a word of thanks as a part of the worship service.

Because Connie Wooten was going to be baptized, I made sure those arrangements were also in place. I sent a midweek notice to our members that we were going to have the baptism and that Connie was the one to be baptized. Amazingly, there had been no objection, and there were several e-mails and phone messages of approval.

Connie had been reinstated in her job at the motel. But we had also hired her at Incarnation to help with the internal maintenance of the facility—cleaning, sweeping, mopping, washing, and taking out the trash. That had been a part of Otis Huntington's job. We allowed Connie to work it around her motel responsibilities. With the combined employment, she would be making enough to live on.

I had gotten to the church so early that it gave me an opportunity to reflect on the week gone by. As I thought about it all, I became somewhat overwhelmed. Not only did I feel safe in my position as pastor but also appreciated. Questions arising from the incarnation challenge and what I had done for Tyler and Connie Wooten seem either to have been forgotten or accepted as appropriate. The Belvedere City Council had fired Police Chief Clyde Matthews and had referred to the district attorney action against Mike Troutman and the others who had damaged Connie Wooten's trailer and threatened her life.

I finally blocked out my reverie and began to check my notes for the sermon. I also wondered how many people would show up for the first class on discipleship I planned to teach in the fellowship hall following the service and wanted to be sure I was prepared for that. I felt a catch in my stomach as I remembered the disaster of the last time I had tried something like this and no one showed up other than the Stoners with their mixed vote. *Well, this is a different time,* I told myself, hoping I really believed it.

As the morning progressed, I looked out in the parking lot to make sure Connie Wooten's little car had arrived. It would be humiliating if, after all the plans for her baptism, she didn't show up. I expelled a sign of relief when she pulled into her designated employee parking space. Later I pecked into the sanctuary and found it filled with a goodly number of folks, including Philip Treadway!

It was only then that a lightning bolt of irony hit me. I realized what happened between those of us at Incarnation Church and Connie Wooten could become a repeat of the failure of our relationship with Otis Huntington or a redemption of that failure. The parallels between the two situations almost seemed orchestrated by God to put us to the test.

The church had hired each of these people to do maintenance work. Each was needy and very alone. Neither was able to dress as well as our more affluent members. Both provided excuses to those who would look down on them— Otis because he committed suicide, Connie because her son had killed some and wounded others.

My mind swung back to things I had said at the

memorial service for Otis:

"Why didn't we minister to him?

"We're an affluent church, yet Otis lived in a rent-assisted apartment. We go out to fine restaurants, but Otis got by on food stamps. We have our social circles. However, Otis's best friend was his little dog, Skeeter.

"Is it possible that we, in our comfort and prestige, never let Otis join the club? Is it possible that we worshiped with Otis every week but never invited him into our lives? Is it possible that he embarrassed us?"

Would I be asking the same questions concerning Connie Wooten some day?

In the worship service this morning, we would be welcoming Connie Wooten into the body of Christ that we call Incarnation Church. Thus, we were facing something in addition to the incarnation challenge—it was the Otis challenge. Would we accept Connie as one of us, despite her low self-esteem, meager income, and inability to dress in the manner of the more affluent members? Would we love and care for her as we did not do for Otis? It was something to ponder.

In basically fifteen days' time, things had come full circle for Incarnation Church.

As she came forward to be baptized, predictably Connie's plain cotton dress was conspicuous in its contrast to the way other Incarnation women were dressed. She had obviously not been to a hairdresser. She wore no makeup to speak of. And she looked scared stiff!

Nonetheless, the baptism went well. The congregation applauded her confession of faith. People swarmed around her to welcome her into the flock. She graciously accepted their words and actions with a shy smile.

To that point, it had been a great day at Incarnation Church, but how many would accept my invitation to come into the fellowship hall to talk about Christian discipleship? I was frankly anxious based on my experience of only two Sundays ago.

We had just installed a coffee station outside the fellowship hall where people could gather for something to drink and snack on after church. It was a good meeting place for those in no hurry to leave and a great opportunity to welcome newcomers and visit with them. Today there was a crowd at the coffee station, with Paul Rivers and his welcome team in charge. How many would come into the fellowship hall?

To my great pleasure, some eighty or so people showed up for my teaching. They seated themselves without fanfare and had eager looks on their faces. It was a good start.

Incarnation Church had begun to live up to its name.

Epilogue

As the weeks went by, a number of Bible study groups sprang up at Incarnation Church. Clifton Stoner became the leader of one of the groups. It met in his home.

The discipleship course in the hour following worship on Sunday mornings increased in attendance.

A newcomers' class was begun for the people who had recently been attracted to the church. Connie Wooten and Philip Treadway were regular in attendance. Treadway asked a lot of questions.

Steve Long was pleased with what was happening at Incarnation Church. He truly believed that an increasing number of its members were coming to see what incarnating Christ in their everyday lives meant in thought and action. But there was still running around in the back of his mind the idea of going elsewhere and planting a church of people who, from the very beginning, were committed to being Christ to their world.

About the Author

Harry C. Griffith is an attorney by education, graduating from the University of Mississippi Law School as editor-in-chief of the *Mississippi Law Journal* and winner of the Phi Delta Phi Award as Outstanding Law Graduate. After serving in the Army JAG Corps, he became a corporate attorney and then executive, rising to the position of vice president–administration before accepting God's call into full-time Christian work as a layperson.

He founded the Bible Reading Fellowship in the United States in 1971 and served as its president for twenty-seven years. He was also executive director of the Anglican Fellowship of Prayer for eleven years and executive officer during the formation years of the Anglican Mission in America. He was a cofounder of Faith Alive, a lay witnessing ministry, and Adventures in Ministry, a lay ministry organization.

He has had more than twenty books published on a wide range of subjects: prayer, Bible study, evangelism, lay ministry, and marriage. His publishers include Tyndale, Zondervan, Eerdmans, and A. R. Mowbray (England).

Harry has been called a Christian entrepreneur because of his varied and creative ministries over the years. He is a speaker, writer, teacher, poet, lawyer, business executive, husband, father, grandfather, and founder of several Christian and business organizations. He has also held a wide range of positions in civic, service, business, and political organizations.